The Man Who Wanted To Drink Up The Sea

The Man

Who Wanted

To Drink

Up The Sea

Pan Bouyoucas

Cormorant Books

Canada Council for the Arts | Conseil des Arts du Canada

ONTARIO ARTS COUNCIL
CONSEIL DES ARTS DE L'ONTARIO

The publisher gratefully acknowledges the support of the Canada Council for the Arts and the Ontario Arts Council for its publishing program. We acknowledge the financial support of the Government of Canada through the Book Publishing Industry Development Program (BPIDP) for our publishing activities.

Printed and bound in Canada

LIBRARY AND ARCHIVES CANADA CATALOGUING IN PUBLICATION

Bouyoucas, Pan
The man who wanted to drink up the sea / Pan Bouyoucas.

ISBN 1-896951-92-9

I. Title.

PS8553.O89M36 2006 C813 .54 C2005-906945-7

Cover design: Angel Guerra/Archetype
Cover image: Carmelo Bongiorno/Getty Images
Author photo: Marie-Reine Mattera
Text design: Tannice Goddard/Soul Oasis Networking
Printer: Friesens

CORMORANT BOOKS INC.
215 SPADINA AVENUE, STUDIO 230, TORONTO, ON CANADA M5T 2C7
www.cormorantbooks.com

The Man

Who Wanted

To Drink

Up The Sea

CURIOUS EYES READING *these lines in search of new adventures and thrills: this is the account of the strange journey Lukas of Montreal embarked on to find the girl he had abandoned back in Greece.*

He wanted to tell her: "I'm sorry." Which is strange enough for a Greek. Ever since that Oedipus of Thebes, Greeks act as if admitting the slightest blunder would cost them both their eyes.

Lukas might have given one. Not that he did not value his eyes. "Little everyday miracles," he called the things they showed him every day. "When I'm under the weather, a woman has only to smile to me," he would say, "and I see life beckoning me again, full of delights and possibilities. That's a miracle, no?"

Alas, the girl he was looking for died before he could tell her how sorry he was for the pain he had caused her, and no smile could cheer him up.

Then he heard how, over the centuries, the attitudes towards dreams have been more or less the same all over the planet: there is the land of the living and the land of the dead, and between them the bridge of the sleeper's mind where they meet at night.

This is the story of one such meeting.

1

THE FIRST TIME Zephira made his heart flutter, Lukas was eleven years old. Zephira was also eleven years old. They were at the primary school in Aghia Marina, the old harbour of the Greek island of Leros.

Lukas's eraser had fallen off his desk, bounced on the floor and come to rest at the girl's feet.

Zephira was hunched over her notebook. With knitted brow and lips pressed together, she was concentrating on the latest test concocted by their sixth-grade teacher, a stern man, tall, bony and straight, nicknamed the Radar because his pupils had come to believe that the large ears sticking out of his head could capture their innermost thoughts.

When Lukas got off his seat and onto the floor to retrieve his eraser from under Zephira's desk, her thighs were splayed out under her navy blue skirt, revealing at their junction a triangle of white cotton.

Lukas had always liked Zephira best among the girls in his class. He liked her best because she had the haughtiest gait and the fleshiest lips. But after he caught a glimpse of her inner thighs, his feelings for her transmuted into a sensation akin to the bouts of fever that had plagued him until he had his tonsils out. This bout, however, was not accompanied by shivering or nausea, only by some trouble swallowing. And by illusions. He was under the impression that all life outside the girl had vanished. That what he had glimpsed within the confines of her skirt appeared everywhere he looked.

He never finished the test. During recess he did not play with the boys in the schoolyard. He withdrew to a corner and watched from a distance the only sign of life that remained in his universe: two scrawny legs jumping rope, unaware of the cataclysm they had unleashed.

After recess, as soon as he was back in his classroom, Lukas pushed his eraser off his desk.

It took him so long to find it that the Radar asked him what he was doing down on all fours again.

Lukas stammered while a blush spread over his face.

"Don't mutter," said the Radar. "Speak clearly — like a man. What are you doing on all fours?"

Nestor, the priest's son, said: "Photographing Zephira's knickers."

There was a titter around the room.

His face aflame, Lukas shut his eyes and called for help

from the Lord, the Lord's mother and all the saints to whom he had lit a candle. He wanted them to whisk him away, right then, to the middle of the Sahara desert.

When he opened his eyes again, the Radar was holding his ruler and motioning to him to step forward.

He whacked the boy five times on the palm of each hand. Lukas held back his tears and sat out the rest of the day, still as a stone. But after they left school, he knocked Nestor down, sat astride him and filled his mouth with earth.

Never again did he speak to the priest's son. Never again did he dare meet Zephira's gaze. He even changed directions when he saw her. Then he would spend the rest of the day fantasizing: Zephira was about to change into her nightgown or take a bath, and he was the Invisible Man.

2

THE SECOND TIME Zephira made his heart flutter, Lukas was seventeen years old. Zephira was seventeen too. But she no longer lived in Aghia Marina; she had moved to Lakki, Leros's new port.

Lakki is the biggest natural harbour in the Mediterranean. After the Italians bought the thirteen Dodecanese islands from the Turks in 1912, Mussolini decided to build in Lakki the naval base from which he planned to recapture some of the glory of Ancient Rome. Because of that dream Leros was bombarded so heavily during World War II — first by the Royal Air Force, to drive the Italians away; then by the Luftwaffe, to drive the British away; then again by the Royal Air Force, to drive the Germans away — that most of the natives who survived the ordeal thought of nothing but emigrating. To keep the menfolk from leaving in droves for jobs abroad, the Greek government converted some of the port installations into an insane asylum which eventually employed half of the island's adult population. Since the end of primary school, Zephira had worked as a maid at the residence of the asylum's director.

Lakki was situated five kilometres from the old harbour of Aghia Marina. To Zephira though it seemed a continent away and she came to Aghia Marina to visit her parents only three or four times a year.

Zephira's father was a fisherman who spent most of his free time playing cards at the Aghia Marina seafront café where Lukas now worked with his own father. There, every three or four months, he caught sight of the girl talking to her father in all her adolescent bloom and his face blazed with embarrassment, convinced that she had not forgotten the eraser incident and that it had damaged relations between them beyond repair.

Some say that nothing stimulates hatred like humiliation. In Lukas's case, he cherished every image that the girl still stirred in him. Although months would pass without him seeing her, it took only a glimpse of a pair of panties for such images to descend upon him again, rouse his thoughts and bewitch him. His hatred was directed at the priest's son.

Nestor had gone on to secondary school and often dropped by the café with his new friends, full of stories about gigantic penises and immense vaginas. To show that his stories were not the product of his imaginings, he kept a sprig of fresh basil behind his right ear. He chewed on it, he said, to rid his breath of the smell of pussy.

Lukas was convinced that the only hairy cracks Nestor had ever licked were his own armpits. The sprig of basil was merely meant to distract attention from his serpent's eyes which were always on the lookout for someone to deride or humiliate. Lukas never returned Nestor's greetings, never waited on his table. "You serve the Devil's grandson," he would tell his father, paraphrasing one of Leros's oldest adages: "Son of a priest, grandson of the Devil."

Aris, the butcher's son, was his only friend. Like Lukas he had stopped his studies after primary school to work at his father's shop. Together they spent their free time reading, rereading or discussing their beloved Illustrated Classics. They were the only publications they could afford and the most entertaining. Some recounted fantastic voyages that would cast a glow over the whole week ahead. The two boys would lift their eyes from their pages only to gaze at the sea and vow to leave their godforsaken island as soon as they could apply for their own passports.

The Illustrated Classics were delivered by boat every Saturday morning. On Saturday nights, when Lukas's mother begged him until "hair grew on her tongue," as she claimed, to accompany her to one feast or another — where there would be scores of marriageable girls — she got as much sympathy from him as from the icon of the Virgin Mary, whom she asked every night in her prayers to cure her boy.

She reasoned that if, at the age of seventeen, he still found pictures of musketeers and supermen in tights more attractive than girls, surely he was an impotent or a pansy. Even his grandmother, who always defended Lukas and often slipped him a few drachmas for buying books, became concerned. On Saint Irene's day, her namesake saint, she insisted that he come with her to the church and to the feast that followed.

Lukas adored his grandmother and never refused her anything. At the feast, when she asked him to accompany her in a round dance, he jumped to his feet the way he used to jump at school when the Radar called out his name.

Soon other dancers joined them. Zephira was one of them.

In every life there are a few moments suspended in time and space when every detail is held in the memory as though tattooed on the brain. That evening proved to be such a moment for Lukas.

Zephira still carried herself with a natural haughtiness, her head held high. Only now its crown of dark and curly hair was spread loosely around it, exuding as much sensuality as did her fleshy lips and her slender body, fully developed at seventeen and with a touch of the animal in it.

"She's a true Amazon," the men sighed.

The women sniffed. "She's just a maid. And probably the shrink's plaything."

Lukas was so troubled by the girl's presence so close to him that he never knew how he came to find himself alone with her after the dance, in a deserted spot on the seashore.

But to his dying day, he would recall the splash of the little waves that carried the full moon to their feet.

Zephira spoke for a while, without once mentioning primary school. But Lukas could hear nothing but the rush of the sea. As it rolled across the pebbles, then retreated, it seemed to whisper to the land, "You're mine. You're mine." And at every roll he swore that at the next one he would take the girl in his arms and devour the lips he ached for. But no matter how often the surf pounded the beach, he could not get up the nerve to even look at Zephira. And when his father appeared from the darkness to tell him it was time to go home, he let himself be dragged away like a drowning boy.

When he reached the house, Lukas learned that his mother had sent his father after him. That infuriated his grandmother and she berated her daughter for not rejoicing that her son had finally shown an interest in a girl.

Her daughter retorted: "Let him flirt. I want him to flirt. But with a girl of good family, not a fisherman's daughter, and a maid at that, looking for an idiot to make her pregnant so he'll marry her without receiving a dowry."

At first Lukas was grateful that his father had rescued him from his despair. But after he went to bed, his heart sank as he realized that he had abandoned Zephira all alone, on the seashore, and he was overwhelmed by shame.

During the days that followed not even his grandmother's soothing words could rouse him. Lest he bump into Zephira at the café, he told his father that he had sprained a knee while dancing and kept to his room. From there he sent telepathic messages, as he had seen it done in his Illustrated Classics, urging the girl to write and tell him that she held no grudge and was willing to give him a second chance. The only news he had though was that the director of the asylum had been transferred to another part of Greece and had taken his young maid with him.

3

THE THIRD TIME Zephira made his heart flutter, Lukas was fifty-eight years old. Zephira was still seventeen. The meeting occurred ten thousand kilometres from their native island and forty years after Lukas had left it to escape the torments of memory, do his military service, then emigrate.

He immigrated to Canada, where he learned English and French, worked at odd jobs, "saved a bean here and a bean there," as the Leros saying goes, then took a wife, fathered a daughter, and opened one of Montreal's better known seafood restaurants. He worked six days a week, from noon till midnight, but on the seventh, the time he spent with his daughter was enough to relieve the strains of routine and fill him anew with gladness towards all things. The memory of the few moonlit moments when two young hearts destined never to merge had beat in time with the breath of the sea had dimmed, along with that of the island that had borne them. Only one thing could bring them into focus again: music from Leros, heard by chance on the radio or at a community feast. It was never more than one song, but from that one song arose a whole island. The quayside in front of his father's café. The smiling sea beyond. The cries of the gulls overhead. The branches of orange trees weighed down every fall with thousands of little suns, as his grandmother called their ripe fruit. The almond trees whose flowering every spring made her sing:

When the almond trees bloom
Even grannies itch for a groom.

He saw each one of them and was moved to tears. Until the memory of his last dance with his beloved grandmother flooded back as well, bringing with it the memory of the girl he had abandoned on the seashore, in the middle of the night. While more recent events blurred in just a few days, that memory remained as sharp as if it had happened yesterday and always overwhelmed him with a rush of shame, he who did not have much to feel shameful about, as a man, a husband, a father, an employer, or a citizen. And in his shame he was astounded every time at how a kiss he had never given could obsess him so much and for so long, when he could hardly remember most of the ones he had given.

The third time Zephira made his heart flutter, Lukas was asleep beside his wife and dreaming.

He was standing on a pebbly shore. To his left was the wide expanse of a slack sea which the first light of the sun was beginning to illuminate. To his right was a mountain, rising like a monster from the deep to salute the dawn of a new day. A leviathan the colour of steel and as sterile and barren, except for the few wild plants growing on its back. Bushes of oregano and thyme and caper which conjured up vague images: him helping his grandmother pick their leaves or buds, climbing to the spots she could not reach.

There was no one else in sight, not even a gull to be heard, only the movement, continuous and gentle, of the little waves rolling on the pebbles. As he gazed at them, a strange sensation came over him: no one was waiting for him, he had nothing to do and all the time in the world to watch the splendour of dawn breaking over the one thing he missed in Montreal — the sea.

That thought had hardly crossed his mind when a dolphin jumped out of the water and flopped at his feet. A big black dolphin that began to shake and wiggle. And as it shook and wiggled, its shape changed and protrusions shot out of its body. An arm. Another arm. Two legs. A head. The head of a girl seventeen springs young, with Zephira's crown of dark curls.

Lukas woke with a start.

In the dark silence of his Montreal bedroom, his wife was sleeping peacefully by his side, in her usual fetal position, her breathing soft and shallow.

What a strange dream, he thought. He found it so enigmatic, especially since it was the first time he had seen Zephira in his dreams, that he played it back in his head until he realized that he had abandoned the girl once again.

The rest of that night, he lay forlorn in his bed, overwhelmed by the feeling of shame that had haunted him like an itch he could not scratch ever since his one moment of cowardice poisoned his memory of the classmate he had loved in secret long after the scrapes of primary school had disappeared from his knees. During the two years of his military service, in the mountains of Epirus, on the Albanian border, when his body longed for a woman, that poisoned memory came back to haunt him every night. During the year that followed, spent waiting on tables in Athens while his application for emigration was being processed, he set out several times in search of the girl, to tell her how sorry he was, but never found her. After he landed in Canada, he was so caught up in the grip of life and circumstances that Zephira's memory became a dim shadow from a distant past that had nothing to do with the trials, tribulations and triumphs of his new life. Whenever he felt the anguish of that memory revive, he removed it from his thoughts by a simple act of the will, recovering his peace of mind with the resilience of the young and the adventurous.

But Lukas was no longer young and in the grip of life. The feeling of shame lingered inside him all of the day that followed. It was only a dream, he would say; but in vain. To free himself of it, he thought of sharing his burden with someone, anyone. But he felt so ashamed of what he had done at seventeen that he still could not talk about it at fifty-eight. He concluded that his was one of those obsessions that must seem ridiculous to those who do not suffer from them, and condemned himself to endure his secret all alone.

The following night, when he slipped back into his marriage bed, he promised himself not to awake when Zephira appeared again. Then he waited to be led away to her through the doors that only sleep could open.

4

ZEPHIRA REAPPEARED EIGHT days later. Eight endless days during which Lukas awoke every morning and went to sleep every night with the Amazon uppermost in his mind.

She reappeared on a quayside much like that found in the old port of Montreal on summer weekends: one teeming with strollers, skateboarders and roller-skaters, musicians, clowns, jugglers, fire-eaters and sword-swallowers, palm readers and portraitists. Many had spiked hair, dog collars and studs, rings and outsize safety-pins hanging from different parts of their bodies, and tattoos so intricate that their skin looked like Oriental rugs.

How Leros has changed, Lukas reflected, thinking that he was back on his native island.

Zephira was seated at a desk similar to the desks they had in primary school. But she was seventeen, her loosened hair was spread around her head, and a crowd had gathered to watch her write in a notebook.

She wrote slowly and with a seraphic expression, as if in a state of grace. When she finally raised the pencil from the page, a letter appeared in the air, above her head:

I

The crowd gasped, then broke into exuberant applause. The girl bowed her head, put aside a strand of hair from her face, then stooped over the page again.

The crowd watched with voiceless amazement as she drew another letter with the slowness and application of a schoolgirl.

a

There was another round of applause. Children too young to read wanted to move on and were hissed to silence by their elders.

Lukas was itching to talk to Zephira. But the ring of spectators had thickened as more strollers had stopped to watch, and he did not want to spoil their fun. He decided to wait until the girl had finished her show, and shifted his gaze to the space above her head.

m

Another exclamation rose from the crowd.

"I am," some murmured, full of admiration, as they clapped their hands.

I am what? Lukas wondered.

The girl was stooped again over her notebook, and the crowd was once again staring, transfixed, at the space above her head, waiting in fascination for the next letter.

Lukas too waited with bated breath for the rest of the sentence, as if it were addressed to him.

Then Nestor appeared.

Like Zephira, he had not aged a day since the last time Lukas had seen him. He had a sprig of basil behind his right ear and a finger pointed at Lukas. Next to him stood Lukas's mother. While the Devil's grandson watched with a smug expression on his face, as if he were finally avenging himself for the earth Lukas had stuffed in his mouth, she said to her son, beside herself with rage: "So there you are, you pigheaded fool, still running after that; may Charon run her into the ground! But I'll kill her first and go to hell rather than let her get you into her pants; may they fill with as many worms as the tears I've shed because of that son-stealing slut!"

Lukas felt his blood rush to his head and he woke up.

His wife was sleeping peacefully by his side, in her usual fetal position.

Fortunately, the day had begun to dawn. He rolled out of bed, softly so as not to awake his wife. He went into the kitchen and made himself a cup of coffee, cursing his old schoolmate for bringing his mother to the quayside and forcing him to leave Zephira in the lurch once again. Then he lit a cigarette and wondered about Zephira's writing in the sky. Was it meant for him? If so, how was she planning to end it?

Ach, if only his mother had not interfered. Through the years, he had often dreamt of his grandmother, much less of his father, but never of his mother.

"She really picked the time to turn up in my dreams," he muttered. "I hope she won't come back tomorrow."

5

THE FOLLOWING NIGHT, Lukas had hardly fallen asleep when Yolanda, his wife, woke him to ask him if he was all right. He was moaning, she said, and crying out a name.

Lukas swallowed hard, then asked in his confusion what name did he cry out.

"Zephira. Who is she?"

"A girl from primary school, back in Leros."

Yolanda did not pry any further.

She was a Greek born and raised in Montreal who taught history at a local high school. The first time she had heard of Leros was back in her college days, in the late sixties, when the Greek junta had turned the island into a penal colony for leftist intellectuals and other dissidents. She had not met Lukas yet, so she had to look up the island in her books. Leros's only claim to fame, they said, was that it had been the domain of Artemis, the goddess of the hunt, also associated, as a complement to the sun god Apollo, with the moon. But it did not have one temple to show for it, not even one pedestal.

Leros made the headlines once more, in the eighties, again for reasons even its most chauvinistic inhabitants could not take pride in.

The scandal broke out when a documentary broadcast on the American television program *60 Minutes* revealed to the world the appalling medieval conditions of the inmates of its insane asylum and the disappearance of three million dollars given it for renovations by the European Union. Yolanda concluded that her husband had good reason not to mention his native island too often or give its name to his restaurant; in this he differed from most Greeks and other exiles who had fallen victim to the deceptions of nostalgia, transmuting into a heaven the purgatory they had come from.

Lukas's establishment was called "Thalassa." The sea. Because it was a seafood restaurant and because that word, one of the oldest in the Greek language, was still to him one of its most beautiful.

Thalassa.

He always pronounced each syllable separately. Was he aware of it? Yolanda never pointed it out, lest he stop doing it. Because whenever he did that, his features changed as if at each syllable a wave of blissful well-being washed away a decade off his face and, for a fleeting moment, he was a young boy again, back where the sea still reigned supreme with her consort the sun over his existence and he saw in her more illusions than realities.

These were the only moments she saw Lukas get sentimental about his childhood. Then, a few days ago, he started to reminisce about his grandmother:

"She made me my first sailor's uniform. I was four or five. Every Sunday I'd put on that uniform and she'd take me to Lakki. The Italians had built the port of Lakki, and its streets, unlike those of Aghia Marina, were wide and flat. There, my grandmother would rent me a tricycle, and for an hour, up and down the harbour front I sped — I was convinced — faster than the wind. After the ride, my grandmother always treated me to a lemonade and a shoeshine."

He closed his eyes.

"I remember that shoeshine every time the guys wash my restaurant's windows or wipe a table or the counter. I sit nearby, pretending to be doing my bookkeeping, but my eyes are shut."

He opened his eyes.

"What can I say? When they're wiping those surfaces squeaky clean, the goosebumps that run over my skin pale in comparison with the ripples of pleasure the shoeshine man of Lakki used to send through my body."

Yolanda imputed this sudden burst of nostalgia to the excitement stirred by the upcoming birth of their first grandchild. Lukas was reminiscing about his grandmother, she reasoned, because he was about to become a grandfather himself. But two days later, at the baby shower, Lukas, who could never listen to Greek music sitting down, sat out every dance and hardly said a word to anyone — he who like most Greeks enjoyed conversation with his fellows more than anything else in life. Yolanda would squint now and then at her handsome husband, usually so full of love for life and its pleasures that scores of women had tried to seduce him away from her, and she would tell herself: For years he has wished for a grandchild. Now that his daughter is about to give birth, he has realized that he's no longer the young ram he once was.

The little incident that occurred after they left the baby shower clinched her diagnosis. Lukas stopped on the sidewalk, a look of panic in his eyes: he could not remember where he had parked his car. During the days that followed she noticed in him a growing nostalgia for his native island and saw in this the first glimmering of old age.

First he bought a CD of old songs from Leros and played it every morning until he left for work. Then, when Irene, their daughter, came with her husband for Sunday dinner, he brought an octopus and insisted on showing them how, as a child, he beat and rubbed them forty times against a hard surface to tenderize their meat. After that demonstration, he wanted to grill the octopus as he grilled them back at his father's café before serving them in small pieces with every glass of ouzo.

"The house will stink," Yolanda protested.

Lukas took the Hibachi out in their backyard.

It was late January, the backyard was covered with snow, and the temperature had dipped to minus fifteen degrees Celsius. Yet there he stood, roasting the octopus and telling his wife through the window:

"This spring I'll plant a bougainvillea there."

Yolanda remarked that a bougainvillea would not survive a Montreal winter. Still he added: "I'll also plant a fig tree. I'm not paying ninety-nine cents for a fig. Never paid for a fig in my life. Just picked them off trees. Maybe I'll plant an almond tree too."

He had never said so many things together about plants and planting in all the years she had known him. Moreover, during the meal, he only talked of the smells of jasmine, thyme and oregano that filled the air of Leros every night as if he had just returned from there.

"And the sea," he added with a sigh. "The sea."

That is why Yolanda did not pry any further when he told her that the name he had called in his sleep was that of a girl he had known in primary school, back in Leros. She loved to worm secrets out of people, but that night she let her husband go back to sleep, secure in the knowledge that he had told her the truth.

6

YOLANDA'S HANDSOME HUSBAND did not go back to sleep.

The following morning, when he drove to work, he felt heavy, his mind dull, full of confused ideas.

He arrived at his restaurant before everyone else, made himself a cup of coffee, then called Leros. To find out whether Zephira had returned there or given any indication of her whereabouts.

First he called the island's mayor. Who told him that Zephira had never returned to Leros and that her parents, like Lukas's, were dead. Lukas asked the mayor if he remembered the name of the first director of the psychiatric hospital in Lakki. Maybe he could give him a clue of Zephira's whereabouts.

"He too has passed away," the mayor replied. "I know because he visited us two summers ago. He had only three months to live and he wanted to see Leros one last time."

Lukas called the priest.

By now Nestor's father had passed away, and his successor was an old classmate of Lukas and Zephira's.

"Of course I remember the Amazon," he said. "I fantasized about her until I got my by-pass."

"Has she ever sent you money for a memorial service for her parents?"

"More often than you have."

"Then you know where she lives."

"It was always a five-dollar bill. That's all I remember."

"You mean she has stopped sending you money?"

"She didn't last year."

"What kind of dollars were they? Canadian? American? Australian?"

"The kind you couldn't buy six candles with. And that cheapskate wanted a full-fledged service. Leros is no longer cheap, you know. What do they charge for a memorial service in Montreal these days?"

"I don't know. I'm not in the business of shovelling smoke."

Lukas concluded that Zephira too had passed away. And she had passed away recently. That is what she was about to tell him with those letters that appeared over her head. "I am dead (that is how I could finally find you) and willing to give you a chance to redeem yourself." Or something like that. Didn't his grandmother believe, as did the ancient Greeks, that the dead use dreams to communicate with the living? Could he turn down her offer and grieve at heart again over something he did not do but should have done?

Thus he meditated all of that morning, pondering and brooding over that question as if some dreadful punishment would befall him if he turned down dead Zephira's offer.

Then came the noon crowd: a welcome distraction. By the time the restaurant emptied again, just his envisaging of such a possibility — going after Zephira in his dreams because his grandmother believed that possible — seemed so ludicrous that he could hardly believe that he had contemplated it.

"Ach, what silly stuff I'm thinking," he muttered to himself. "Man will clutch at straws. As if there were such things as spirits and ghosts — bah!"

He poured himself a glass of wine and called his pregnant daughter to see how she was doing. Her voice sufficed to eliminate the bad from his memory and magnify the good. And by the time the evening crowd arrived he was in such high spirits again that he did not give another thought to Zephira and her ominous half sentence. But after he closed his restaurant, on his way to his car he bumped into a group of seventeen-year-old girls. Instantly the whole of his existence was brought together again in the image of its one moment of cowardice.

He thought: Some dead, you can't just bury, say a little prayer to and forget. Unless I make peace with the Amazon, her ghost will haunt my waking hours as well as my sleep. It would only take the sight of a seventeen-year-old girl to bring her out of the shadows again.

7

WHEN HE GOT home that night, Lukas looked so woebegone that Yolanda, in a tone that allowed no reply, said to him: "Spring break is in a month. I know Montrealers will starve if you skip one day's work, still I'm taking you to Cuba for a week."

Lukas told himself that he would not make it through another week let alone a month, unless he found the creature of his torment and settled their accounts once and for all. But how could he do that?

The next day, he looked like a man condemned to drink up the sea. Gone was his outgoing personality that had always made his employees feel that, like a family, they were preparing dinner for their guests. Because to Lukas's eyes, his restaurant was an extension of his house where he could receive friends and engage them in conversation over a good meal. For that reason those waiters who had quit — most of them students at the National Theatre School or unemployed actors — kept coming back, not as celebrities but as visiting relatives, and he was always among the first on their list of people they invited to the premiere of a play or a film. The restaurant's regular patrons — which included writers, journalists and members of the various levels of government, whose careers Lukas followed daily in the press — also felt part of their extended family.

Judy Yamada was one of those regular patrons. An anthropologist in her early forties, she came to the Thalassa at least once a month with her husband or a colleague from McGill University where she taught. Lukas always treated her with the same casualness he showed towards everyone else. That evening, however, he seemed tense when he told her: "The ancient Greeks believed that the dead communicate with the living through dreams. What about the Japanese?"

For the first time in all the years she had known him, Judy noticed that Lukas truly looked his age that night. She made no mention of it, only saying: "Over the centuries, the attitudes towards dreams have been more or less the same all over the planet. There's the land of the living and the land of the dead, and between them the bridge of the sleeper's mind where they meet every night. To this day, in many parts of the world, it's believed that the soul of the sleeper goes out and wanders — often to visit those dead — while its human habitation, the body, sleeps. They never wake a person suddenly in case his spirit fails to get back into his body in time."

"What do *you* believe?"

"I believe that, like our oldest fears, our oldest dreams are with us forever."

Lukas put on his coat and went out for a walk.

It was a long shot, he thought as he strolled round the block. But he had nothing to lose and much to win. First, however, he should take the necessary measures to make sure that Yolanda would not hear him talk to the girl. He should also make sure not to wake when he saw Zephira again.

The next morning he called on his family doctor and asked him for sleeping pills. Like Judy Yamada, the doctor took a good look at him and noticed, for the first time in all the years he had known Lukas, that he truly looked his age.

At the pharmacy, while he waited for the pharmacist to fill the prescription, Lukas thought of spending the night in a hotel room where no one would hear what he said in his sleep. But what would he tell his wife now that she had heard him call a woman's name? Though he could hardly bear his anguish much longer, he decided to wait two more days. The following Monday, like the first Monday of every month, he was to play poker with his friends. Yolanda never waited up for him on those nights.

He loved poker and would have accepted any engagement which could have given him a few hours' escape from thought. Yet that Monday he opted out, weary and faint as he was from lack of sleep and in no mood for idle chatter. However, he left his restaurant early, as he always did on poker nights, and spent the rest of the evening at a café, drinking no less than three glasses of wine to deaden his inward agitation. When he finally arrived home, with the irrevocable conviction that there would be no joy for him again until he found Zephira and made peace with her, all the lights of his house were out except the one above the garage door.

It was a cold night. The air was crisp, the sky clear. A wind swished the treetops to and fro. Through the window of the Hasidic study house across the street, black silhouettes of men swayed over their holy books. Lukas too prayed — to find his joy again so he could love and spoil his grandchild as his grandmother had loved and spoiled him. Then he parked his car in the garage, leaving the exterior light on. Should Yolanda awake, he did not want her to know that he was home. Tomorrow, if she woke before he did, he would tell her that he was so tired he could not drag himself to their bed.

Satisfied with his set-up, he settled himself comfortably in his seat, buttoned up his coat to keep himself warm, and swallowed a sleeping pill — his first one ever. Then, his chin drawn deep into the turned-up collar of his coat, he waited for sleep to take him to the girl of his dreams.

The garage was cold and he kept shuddering and falling in and out a doze. But he would not give up. Only one thought occupied his mind, and he was determined to see it through. His teeth chattered and violent spasms shook his body, his eyes were stony and his face without expression, like that of a man resolved upon a dangerous but inevitable journey that could last to the end of his life; he extended a hand, and, his sleep-numbed brain unconscious of the gravity of his gesture, he switched on the engine to turn on the heating system of his car.

8

WHEN HER HUSBAND parked his car in their garage, Yolanda was in bed. But she was not asleep. She was reading. But hard as she tried to concentrate on what she was reading, she could not take in a word. The wine she had consumed that evening kept washing her thoughts back to the man she had dined with and the proposition he had put to her.

In her twenty-nine years as a teacher, Yolanda had had many students. Most of them she had forgotten. Some faces she remembered, but not the names. There were a handful, however, she recalled everything about, particularly the look in their eyes when they listened to her in class. Daniel Bouchard was one of them. He had taken to history like a child to ice cream.

After high school, he went on to college, then university, ringing her up now and then to discuss an assignment, a teacher, or one of the many girls he kept falling in and out of love with. Eventually he obtained a Doctorate in History, got his thesis published, and dedicated the book to "the teacher and mentor who revealed to me and nurtured my vocation." Yolanda was so moved that she invited him to dinner at her husband's restaurant. Daniel arrived with a young woman of Greek descent. During dinner he whispered to Yolanda that he would call her the following day to find out what she thought of her because he was seriously considering marrying her before moving to Chicoutimi, a city seven hundred kilometres north of Montreal, to teach at the local university.

After the young couple left, Lukas told his wife:

"Did you notice how much the girl resembles you?"

"Yes, but she doesn't talk half as much as I do. She hardly said ten words all evening."

"Because she realized Daniel doesn't love her half as much as he loves you."

"I could be his mother."

"He's got a mother."

Daniel Bouchard did not call her the next day to ask her what she thought of his fiancée. He did not call her to invite her to their wedding either, nor to bid her farewell before moving to Chicoutimi. Daniel rang her up again two years later, to tell her that he could not stand Chicoutimi — too homogeneous, too bland, too boring — and had moved back to Montreal. Then he said: "Are you free tonight? I'm working on a new book I'd like to talk to you about."

She suggested Lukas's restaurant.

Daniel said: "These past two years, I've eaten nothing but Greek at home. How about sushi?"

She concluded that he had married the young woman of Greek descent, and when he picked her up at seven, she was surprised to learn that they had broken up the day after their dinner at the Thalassa.

Daniel Bouchard was in his mid thirties now, but his eyes still had the same intense adolescent look every time his eyes fastened on Yolanda's face. A look that made Yolanda feel uneasy now for it stirred in her feelings that had nothing to do with those of a teacher towards a former student. Fortunately, tonight, Daniel did most of the talking.

"I've done a lot of thinking in Chicoutimi," he said. "There wasn't much else to do in the evenings. I thought mostly about the rise of religiosity and religious militancy, and its modern expression — what I like to call sanctimonious terrorism. Maybe it was due to my isolation, but I had the impression that the rest of the world was slipping back to Hypatia's time. I hadn't given her much thought since you first mentioned her name in class, twenty years ago, to tell us about the importance of books. But as I watched the news, I felt sometimes that we were back in 415 A.D., when Hypatia was trying to defend the Alexandrian library with its four hundred thousand books against the mobs of monks who wanted to set fire to it in order to impose one book.

"How is that possible? I kept thinking. The burning of all those books and the imposition of a single one led to ten centuries of darkness, if not more. Why would men want to bring back even ten years of that? If they're searching for spirituality in a materialistic world, God is light, not darkness, and no religion sanctions the systematic use of the murder, injury and destruction so prevalent today. What is it then that truly motivates men to do things that more often than not are alien to the faith they claim to defend?

"I read scores of books and articles on fundamentalism, in the West as well as in the East. I spent hours looking at footage shot throughout the world in the last twenty, twenty-five years. Then one day I saw, back to back, these two news items. The first one was an interview with the pope. When he was asked about reported cases of nuns raped by priests, he replied: 'Don't you think that the irresponsible conduct of man is caused by women?'

"The second item was about eight armed men who had stormed an elementary school in Algeria. They ordered everyone out in the school yard, picked one girl, slit her throat in front of all the other children, then told them: 'Go home now and tell your parents this is what will happen to their daughters if they send them back to school.'

"I looked again at some of the footage I'd seen. The Iranians who occupied the US embassy in 1979 wanted principally to impose a theocracy, to protect their people against American imperialism and Western 'decadence.' Yet most of the men wore T-shirts and jeans. But not the women. Even in pro-American countries, like Saudi Arabia, men have access to everything the Western world has to offer, but their women aren't even allowed to drive a car. I wouldn't give it a second thought if, to preserve their religion and culture, men excised themselves too — or whatever it's called for men. If they too abstained from using the Internet, as Hasidic women in Israel are forbidden to. But it's always women who must be protected. Why? Are they more easily influenced and led astray, driving men, as the pope claims, to act irresponsibly? Even in the US, the explosion of moral righteousness is mostly aimed at sexual issues in general, and women issues in particular. I may be reading too much into this, but I'm almost tempted to say that, at a deep subconscious level, it's the fear of women and their liberation that drove those men to fly planes into the Twin Towers.

"I know, women have often condoned and helped perpetuate the ideologies, laws and measures that subjugate them. But they've been kept so long in the dark that they've forgotten all about the light. Even if a little light did ever get in, their soul would still refuse to believe in it because, at first, that light would be frightening.

"Yolanda, I might be totally off the track. That's why I need your help. Tackling a subject like this one by myself would be like eating with one chopstick. I need a woman's point of view."

His words took her by surprise.

"Why me?"

Was she fishing for a compliment? She blushed before she even got it. And when she got it, it left her at a loss, for she did not know how to interpret it.

"You're the only woman I could see myself spending hours

with, discussing and writing this book," Daniel said. "I'm not only looking for well-researched, cold, academic facts and arguments. I also want to see in my partner's face, you know, some sign of a life being lived, a few marks, that prove she's been there."

He handed her four sheets of typed notes. "Read them first. Think about it. Then call me. Here's my new phone number. I hope you'll call soon. I've been dreaming of such a collaboration for years, but I could not find a topic worthy of you. I hope you'll say yes. It would make me very happy."

Four hours later, Yolanda was trying to read those notes when Lukas drove his car into their garage. But her thoughts were taken more by the motive behind Daniel's proposition rather than its substance. Had he sought her help and collaboration only because she was a historian, she wondered as his words kept going round and round in her head. She had laughed at Lukas's remark about Daniel loving her more than his fiancée, but she had sensed that as well, and was flattered to be desired still, at her age. Now, however, all alone in her bed, that feeling had turned to panic. She would love to work on a book. She was tired of teaching history to kids mainly interested in the Hollywood version of it. This project would help boost her up again. But what if Daniel's motives were not strictly professional?

She let out a deep sigh. Get a grip, for chrissake, she told herself. It was an innocent proposition. Don't let your hormones tell you otherwise.

Yet, when she heard the garage door open, she switched

the bedside light off, as if those hormones and the thoughts they were stoking inside her head were flashing on her face. Only when she heard the garage door shut again did she wonder why Lukas had come home this early tonight. Had something happened? She closed her eyes, the better to hear his footsteps. She would know what to expect from the sound of his footsteps.

As she waited for her husband to come up to their room, her mind began to fill with the sounds of the night and slowly she drifted off to sleep.

9

EVERY NIGHT WHEN Lukas came home, he showered to rid himself of the smell of fish that had settled during the course of the day and evening on his hair, on his skin, on every stitch of his clothing. So, when sleep finally came and he entered that land that appears on no map, he found himself looking for a shower where he could wash before meeting with Zephira.

The city was asleep under a blanket of snow, the streets deserted as on those nights in the dead of winter when the thermometer dips to its lowest levels. The street lamps emitted the only light, feeble and dimly reflected from the drifts; and a fierce wind blew, pelting him with flakes as sharp as little knives that cut into the flesh of his face.

A Boeing was parked at the bus stop across the street from the restaurant where he had spent the better part of his adult life amassing a small fortune which had now lost all meaning in his eyes. A long line of passengers waited to board, stamping their feet to keep warm. He shouted to them — Where could he find a shower? — but they did not hear him. He waved at them, but they did not see him.

His family doctor appeared between the drifts. He shook Lukas's hand and wished him a pleasant journey.

Lukas said: "First I must rid myself of the smell of fish. Where can I find a shower?"

"You have no time for a shower," the doctor replied. "Just take off your coat."

Lukas looked at his coat: it had lost all its buttons but one and was covered with fish scales. Still, he shuddered at the thought of taking it off on such a cold and blustery night. But the line across the street was getting shorter and the plane's engines were rumbling. So he wrenched at his coat's remaining button, shouting: "Wait for me!" But his fingers were too stiff with cold and he could not undo the button. In hopeless rage he tried to tear the coat apart, but the material was too gluey and slippery. The plane started to roll. "Wait for me!" he shouted again, dashing across the street. But the traffic light changed to green and the plane took off and soon vanished in the dark night.

When Lukas lowered his eyes, the bus stop shelter had also vanished. His restaurant too. The entire street. Whichever way he turned he saw nothing but an endless landscape of snowdrifts. Not the slightest glimmer of a light, not the slightest sign of life anywhere.

Damn button.

He waded forward through the snow, struggling and scrambling and calling out Zephira's name. "You have every right to be upset and not to appear when I call," he said. "Three times I've left you in the lurch. I'll come to you. Just give me a sign. I'll do the rest."

He listened closely for a reply, a sign. The night stretched all around him, sunk in ominous silence.

He thought he was about to die a slow death, lost on the icy barrens, when he saw a train of small open cars, much like a roller coaster's, moving across the desolate landscape, dipping sharply up and down the drifts. Human figures were sitting in the cars.

Was it the sign he was hoping for? Was Zephira giving him one last chance?

As the train passed by, he jumped on the first car and found himself sitting next to Elaine Duval, his MNA and one of his oldest customers.

"You poor man," she said. "Your teeth are chattering."

She blew softly into his face to warm him.

"Don't warm him too much," a chorus of voices said behind them. "We want to blow in his face too."

Lukas looked over his shoulder. The other carriages were all occupied by women, but in the dark he could only make out the features of the one sitting right behind him: Mona Davis, a middle-aged actress with a great fondness for ouzo and the philosophy of Tao.

"The Real is Empty and the Empty is Real," she said,

making eyes at him.

Presently the train of little carriages began to climb up the facade of a high-rise building like a caterpillar. When it reached the roof, it rattled on along the narrow rails that ran on the parapets of the rooftop, making sharp turns at the corners, then performing marvellous manoeuvres as it dipped down and up buildings. As it swooped down a skyscraper, Lukas caught sight of the sea. He stood up. The last two times he had seen Zephira, she was near water.

"Stop the train," he said.

But Elaine would not stop the train. "Stay," she said, grabbing his left foot. "I'll give you a Lakki shoeshine."

Lukas tried to wriggle his foot free.

Not one to be rebuffed so easily, Elaine told Mona to grab his other foot.

"No, please no," Lukas begged as they commenced to massage his feet.

"Stop fighting it," Mona said. "It's what your soul is yearning for."

The ripples of pleasure that went through Lukas's body were so strong that he could not move. But he could still speak. So he said: "The soul, yes. But what is the soul?"

The two women looked at him, flabbergasted. "You don't know?"

"Tell me. I'm just a fish peddler. Enlighten me."

The two women let go of his feet. "Sit down," they said.

Lukas jumped off the train.

10

HERE THE GROUND was not covered with snow and the air was warmer. On one side of him, the sea lay as far as he could see, resting, great and peaceful, in the stillness of the dawn. On the other side, there was only sand. And no sign of Zephira. In fact, there was no one around, except for a young man digging with a shovel. Still, Lukas looked at him with delight: the young man was Aris, his best friend from his teenage years. Like Zephira and Nestor, he had not aged a day since Lukas had last seen him.

He thought: For sure Aris will help me find the Amazon. But no sooner had he approached him than his friend handed him a shovel and told him to dig with him.

"Dig for what?" Lukas said.

"The seventh wonder. Have you forgotten? As Schliemann did with Troy, we said, we would go abroad, make a mint, then return and devote our fortune and our remaining years to finding some ruins that our island would be proud of. I have it all in writing. A pledge, signed by you and me, to come back to Leros and look for the temple of Artemis."

Lukas did remember their vow to leave their island, but he had no recollection of a vow to return there to unearth the temple of Artemis. Yet there was the pledge, with his signature on it. To save face, he resorted to a half-lie.

"I didn't forget that pledge," he said. "I simply crossed it out of my mind when I read in the papers that the temple of Artemis included among the seven wonders of the world was erected in Ephesus, not on Leros."

Tears clouded Aris's eyes. He had always been the more sentimental and patriotic of the two.

"We made a hundred plans," Lukas said. "We can't realize them all."

Aris wiped his tears. "They had pictures of the temple in the papers?"

Lukas did not have the heart to compound his half-lie with deceit and hurt his friend still further, should he eventually discover the truth. So he said: "No. They don't know its exact location yet."

"Then it may all be rumours and misinformation, spread by the Turks to rob us of our tourists."

He resumed digging, urging Lukas to dig with him.

"I must talk to Zephira first," Lukas said. "Do you know where I might find her?"

"In the graveyard. One is always sure to find a dead person in her grave. Take the shovel with you; you might need it. And remember me to Zephira."

Along the horizon the sky began to flush bright with the dawn. As Lukas turned to go, a rooster fluttered up from under the sand. Flapping its wings, it picked its way to the edge of the water, then cocked its head towards the horizon to celebrate with its cry the birth of another day.

"Ach!" Lukas said. "He's going to wake my wife!"

With a swing of his shovel Aris chopped off the cock's head. The bird jumped about headless, splattering blood on the pebbles, and ended up in the water. Aris waded in after it, picked it up and started to pluck it, telling Lukas the cock would be cooked by the time he got back.

He looked like a torso floating on a carpet of feathers tinted slightly pink. The ancient torso of an oracle bobbing on the surface of an ocean of mysteries and revelations.

11

WHEN LUKAS TURNED towards the direction Aris had indicated, in a burst, all was transformed into a radiant morning and he saw a row of cypresses, tall, slender and straight, standing guard, in their aristocratic silence, over a row of small round tables with white marble tops. A man was sitting at each table. The men were old and dressed in their Sunday best. They reminded Lukas of the nattily dressed old men who had once frequented his father's café. There was one difference, though. Here, no one spoke. With downcast eyes, the men seemed to be ruminating the dyspeptic broth of their memory, oblivious even to the butterflies that hovered around them like souls bidding farewell to the bodies they had abandoned.

Lukas thought: If this is the graveyard, where are the women? And how can I extract that information from these men without hurting their feelings, in the event they're not dead? No one likes to be mistaken for a cadaver, at that age especially.

He started by greeting the men. When they heard his voice, their faces lit up and they jumped out of their seats, each stretching out his arms to invite him to his table, peppering him with questions: Who was he? Where did he come from? What was he looking for?

When Lukas told them that he was looking for the graveyard, the enthusiasm he had stirred in them vanished as quickly as it had come.

"Why should we know where the graveyard is?" said a corpulent and bull-necked man. "Because we are old?"

Shaking their heads and dispirited, they slumped back listlessly in their seats. A dandy with a goatee and a cane was so irritated that he squashed the butterfly sitting on his table with his gloved fist.

These men are not dead, Lukas concluded. Curiosity is a sign of life and these men are sick with it. So he said: "Gentlemen, forgive me if I've offended you. I'm in such desperate straits that I've forgotten my manners."

Most ignored him. Some again fastened their eyes on him as if he were a drama about to unfold. And one man, a small one with a slight build, seemed amused by his predicament. Why was he in desperate straits, he asked, smiling the smile of someone who had seen much and wished to hear of even worse things.

"I'm about to become a grandfather," Lukas said, hoping this would strike a sensitive chord. "If I don't find the dead girl I'm looking for, I may never live to see my grandchild. It's a long story. I wish I had the time to tell it."

The dandy with the goatee piped up again: "Excuse me, what do I hear? He has no time for our questions, but he doesn't mind wasting what little time we have left with his questions?"

"All you have to do is point to the cemetery," Lukas said. "Is it on the other side of this row of cypresses?"

"Why should it be there?" replied the bull-necked man. "Because we are here, the cemetery shouldn't be far?"

Calmly Lukas said that he mentioned the cypresses because back when he was the same age as the girl he was looking for, cypresses always stood guard like votive columns around graveyards. On the other hand, on the island of Montreal where he now lived, they had lindens and weeping willows. What about here, he said, hoping to extract the information he was seeking with a trick question. What trees did they plant in their cemeteries?

"There he goes again with them cemeteries!"

"Ignore him," said the bull-necked man. "He's nothing but a disappointment."

"A great disappointment," said the others.

"Good!" cried out the dandy with the goatee.

The others looked at him. "What's good about it?"

"Think. What would life be without disappointment? There would be no fear, no self-doubt, no self-discovery.

So be grateful for disappointment. It's the great tutor of mankind," the dandy went on, his voice rising in pitch. "The mother of wisdom. We should be grateful for the cups of bitterness she serves us now and then."

Silence.

Disappointed at the lack of reaction, the dandy said: "Come on, fellows, disprove what I said."

"We have been through that topic more times than to a funeral," said the small man with the slight build.

"His memory is starting to fail," whispered the others, and they were about to slump back in their seats when they saw Lukas turn away. "Where are you going?" they said.

"To find someone who'll give me directions. There should be a waiter here." And, noticing a pavilion, Lukas headed for it, adding: "I hope it's a waitress. I always had more luck with women. All except one, of course."

The men jumped out of their seats, perked up again. "Which one? Please tell us, may the Lord grant you all your wishes. Which woman did you have less luck with?"

"Why should I tell you, when you don't even have the goodness to point to me the way to the cemetery?"

"All ways lead to the cemetery," said the small man with the slight build. "You should know that at your age."

"Jesus. Can't you give me a straight answer?"

"If we do the conversation will be over and you'll leave."

"What? I'm supposed to stand here and entertain you while I'm about to lose my joy?"

He approached the entrance of the pavilion, calling the

waiter, and stopped dead in his tracks. Inside the pavilion, standing in front of a mirror, Nestor, his old nemesis, was putting a fresh sprig of basil behind his ear.

Lukas quickly turned on his heels.

"Look," said the corpulent and bull-necked man. "He doesn't want the waiter to see him."

"Waiter! Waiter!" they all shouted tauntingly.

Lukas begged them to stop. But they would not stop unless he gave them something to talk about. If he did, they said, they would take him themselves to the grave he was looking for.

Now, Lukas knew many stories; his profession required that of him. But no matter how hard he ransacked his brain, he was so shaken by Nestor's reappearance that he could not remember a single one of the hundreds of jokes and anecdotes he had committed to memory.

Taking pity on him, the small man with the slight build said: "Let me help you. Why don't you want the waiter to see you?"

"He'll thwart my every attempt to find that dead girl."

"Why must you find her?"

"I've something to ask of her."

"Wow!" the men said. Then each turned to the one next to him and said: "What would you ask the dead if you could speak to them?"

The question raised their fancy to such an extent that the air was soon filled and buzzing with questions and answers and claims and counterclaims. They were so busy arguing, amidst the swarms of butterflies that circled around them, that Lukas had to pull on their sleeves to remind them of their promise. And when they finally decided to take a moment to show him Zephira's grave, a younger voice pierced the general din with a cockiness much too familiar to Lukas.

"Someone called for the waiter?" it said.

Lukas quickly lifted his coat over his head and turned away.

12

WHEN HE PEEKED out from under his coat again, Nestor was gone, but so were the old men and the cypress trees. Only the road was left, but Lukas no longer knew in which direction he should go. He was about to curse the Devil's grandson, when he caught sight of a woman with a coffin placed upon her head.

The woman was young and plump and she carried the coffin with such ease and grace, not even using her hands to hold it steady on her head, that it seemed no heavier than a pillow. Surely she was heading for the cemetery. Lukas hurried after her and asked her if she knew where Zephira's grave was. Yes, she said, she knew where Zephira's grave was, and he followed her, heaving a sigh of relief.

But his relief was short-lived. An older woman appeared, dressed in black and overwrought with grief. She blocked their way, saying to the young woman carrying a coffin on her head: "Where are you going with the body of my son dressed for all eternity, like a destitute, in his pyjamas?"

Other people appeared, whispering: "In his pyjamas?"

Others whispered back: "That's what she said."

And others: "Imagine that! Sending him to face his Maker in his pyjamas!"

The word bounced from mouth to mouth, growing from a whisper into a rumour, and the rumour — "In his pyjamas?" "In his pyjamas!" — whipped some into a rage and others into hysterical laughter. Arms reaching into the air, the mother of the deceased appealed now to the Almighty for the eternal damnation of her daughter-in-law, while a group of elderly women, like a chorus, clutched their hands over their heads and swayed to and fro, chanting: "In his pyjamas! In his pyjamas!"

The mother: "Such a prince. Always in a suit, even when he was a child. I rue the day he married that spendthrift who squandered all he earned. And in return for the crown of pearls he put on her head, that ungrateful strumpet stints my poor boy even of his tie."

The chorus: "She probably sold it along with his suit to buy herself another dress."

The mother: "But not a black one. No. Not even a veil."

The chorus: "And the way she walks, on such a day. Instead of crossing her hands upon her breasts, she strolls towards the cemetery, fluttering her naked arms and wiggling her hips — you'd think she's in a beauty contest."

The mother: "That's how she bewitched my poor boy. He's not yet laid to rest and she's already back to the tricks of her trade to catch herself another idiot."

The women of the chorus cupped their hands over their mouths and shook their heads at the horror of it all, while some men shouted: "Let's bury her too. In her baby doll."

But other men, probably the widow's relatives, stepped forward to protect her. And soon both sides were trading slurs and insults, filling the air with howls and threats; some women fainted, while others used their hands to fan air into the faces of the unconscious.

There was only one way to break this impasse so that Lukas and the widow could get quickly and safely to the cemetery. He held up his arms and shouted: "The widow has cut off her tongue!"

The crowd fell instantly into a hush.

"If she hasn't cut off her tongue," Lukas continued, "why doesn't she tell us why she has dressed the body of her husband in his pyjamas? We deserve an explanation."

All eyes turned to the widow.

"The first thing he did when he came home from work," she said, "was to change into his pyjamas. I'd beg him to keep his suit on and take me out, but he'd say that all day he looked forward to taking his suit off, because he never felt happier than when he was in his pyjamas."

There was a moment's silence. Then arguments and scuffles broke out again between the widow's relatives, or most of them, and those of the mother-in-law, or most of them, for in each camp there were those who took for the other side's point of view: relatives of the deceased who did not feel it unseemly that he go on his last journey dressed in his pyjamas if, when alive, he preferred them to his suits; relatives of the widow who insisted that a man should be buried in a proper suit, regardless of his dress preferences when he was alive.

Lukas held up his arms again. "Ladies, gentlemen. Let's go settle this matter in the cemetery. This is no place to keep a dead soul waiting."

There was another silence. And while everyone pondered his suggestion, Nestor appeared again.

"Who is this guy?" he said. "And why is he in such a rush to get the deceased to his grave? Could he be the widow's new lover? Look, he has even brought a shovel, to dispose of the body quickly so he can go back to humping that wanton."

These last words created such a stir that catcalls and curses were thrown at Lukas, as well as gobs of spit. He remained calmed though, laid down his shovel, then pulled on the sides of his coat. The material was still gluey and slippery, but his fingers were no longer stiff, and as soon as he pulled, the one remaining button popped.

"Look at the label," he said. "My coat was made in Canada. I'm wearing it still because I've just arrived from there. If I've just arrived from Canada, how could I know the widow?"

Most of those closest to him jumped back as soon as he opened his coat. Some, holding their nose, looked at the label, then said that the coat was indeed made in Canada.

At once Nestor's hated voice rose again. "Get Elaine for references. She knows everyone in Canada."

And to his surprise, who did Lukas see come forward through the crowd? His MNA, Elaine Duval. He gave her his most winning smile and, in the name of their old friendhip, he asked her to tell these good people that he could not possibly know the widow. But Elaine had an ego so big that, scorned as a woman in her attempts to give him a Lakki shoeshine and piqued as a politician by his escape as she was about to lecture him on the soul, she said: "True, that man has just arrived from Montreal — a city where he is well known for having the inclinations of a spider. What else could that smell he carries everywhere with him be but the smell of a philandering spider?" she continued, her voice picking up an oratorical flourish.

"If you could only see him, as I've seen him, threading his way through the tables of his restaurant, eyeing and appraising every victim caught in its web, throwing a bon mot here, making a compliment there, offering a free drink to every female patron past her prime and hungry for a look of appreciation in a man's eyes. But old meat can no longer satisfy his depraved virility, and the worn-out profligate has to go out hankering after younger flesh, even if it means hitting on a poor widow still carrying the coffin of her beloved husband. That, my friends, is a slander which stabs not only our very heart as women, it will also inflict such pain on his poor wife's soul, that for sure it will kill her as he has killed so many others."

Incensed by such evil lies and lurid overstatements, Lukas wanted to respond. But a man, his face sullen and hostile, grabbed him by the lips and said: "Come with us. And take it like a man."

Fortunately, the widow had appreciated Lukas's intervention in her defence and she distracted everyone's attention away from him by shouting to the crowd: "I've had enough. You bury him. His suit is in his top drawer."

Then she was gone, leaving the coffin on the ground, the mother-in-law wailing and saying that only the widow could lay her husband to rest, and everyone else running after the widow, imploring her to come back. Only the Devil's grandson was left. He looked at Lukas confused.

"You're supposed to awake. Wake up!"

A raging anger surged in Lukas as it had done many years ago, outside their old school. He walked towards Nestor, saying: "I took a sleeping pill."

Nestor turned on his heels and ran for his life.

In his haste to catch him, Lukas forgot to pick up the shovel his friend Aris had given him.

13

HE RAN ACROSS fields and over hills; Nestor, younger and swifter of foot, always a few steps ahead. Now that he knew that Lukas had taken a sleeping pill, that rat was going to lead him mercilessly on until its effect wore off. If Lukas failed to catch him and wipe the smugness off his face once and for all, he would have to take another sleeping pill, then another and another, what with smugface hounding him in his dreams, trying to foil his every plan. But how could he get his hands on him? The bastard could still run like the wind, and there he was now flying down a street, through the traffic.

Lukas did not recognize the street at first. How could he, coming from so far? He recognized the surroundings only after he chased Nestor through a large, revolving, glass door and emerged inside the Eaton's department store.

The sly son of a priest had led him back to Montreal!

Eaton's was teeming with people. It was the store's closing sale and thousands had come to take advantage of the bargains. A canal ran down the main floor and the items that were being liquidated floated by on plastic rafts of different colours and sizes, while a loudspeaker blared a description of each one and its new reduced price. At every announcement, a loud roar went up on both sides of the canal and people rushed to the edge of the water as the item floated by under the roving spotlights. Those in need of that item tumbled over one another and jumped into the waist-deep water, some struggling for footing, others wading eagerly towards the prized object, splashing it and spattering themselves in the process. When a fight broke out, the voice from the loudspeaker asked everyone to remain calm, please, because there were enough units to satisfy everyone, while television crews scurried over to catch the images of the drowning and interview those climbing back out of the water, drenched to the skin, clutching their spoils against their chest or holding them up triumphantly, their eyes beaming with pride.

"The Bug Buster," the loudspeaker was now saying. "The most powerful portable vacuum cleaner ever. Will rid you of bugs, rats and all unwelcome guests — for only nine ninety-nine!"

Lukas pushed his way towards the canal. All he had to do was to get hold of a Bug Buster, aim its nozzle at the Devil's grandson and press the button. But as he pushed forward, the crowd withdrew, clasping their noses and saying, "What's that smell?" Thus Lukas found himself alone on the edge of the water with hundreds of eyes glaring at him.

"It's Lukas!" some women cried. They were his neighbours, Voula, Soula and Roula. "Call his wife! He's lost in a store without her!"

Lukas panicked. What will Yolanda think when she finds out that he was at Eaton's instead of that poker game? He had to stop his three neighbours from reaching a phone. So he rushed towards them, and who did he see again, standing in his way? The Devil's grandson and Elaine Duval, swaying with delight and chanting:

Hello, Yolanda, hello!
There's something you ought to know.
Hubby's in dreamland again,
Fanning flames dead long ago.

His head reeling, Lukas thought: I'll never find Zephira.

No sooner had he thought that than the Amazon appeared from nowhere, lifted the Bug Buster off its raft, aimed its nozzle at the singing duo, and sucked Nestor and Elaine off the face of the earth.

A wave of panic went through the crowd and everyone ran for cover. Everyone except Lukas. But Zephira did not so much as glance towards him. She simply dropped the Bug Buster and vanished through a door.

Lukas rushed after her and found himself inside an

immense warehouse filled with boxes piled up on top of each other. Some piles reached to the ceiling. There were rows and rows of boxes, creating long, narrow, dark alleys.

Zephira was nowhere in sight. As Lukas searched for her, faint voices reached him. "Call the police!" they were saying. "Call 911! Get him out of there!" A moment later, footfalls echoed from all sides, heading in his direction. "Track the stench," a voice said.

Lukas took his coat off, he chucked it as far away from him as he could, then he struggled onto a box, then onto another, and another, until he reached the top one.

Below, men were running now through the aisles and converging on his coat.

Lukas jumped onto the next pile, then onto another. Some boxes sank under his feet, some tilted towards one side or the other, but he stumbled ahead with sombre determination until he reached the top of the highest pile, inches from the ceiling.

He peered over the edge of the box he was perched on.

They had found the coat he had left behind as a decoy, and were calling back and forth, on the warehouse floor, like dogs that had picked up a scent.

He had to do something. Sooner or later they would find him and force him to leave Zephira in the lurch again. She would not forgive him this time. But where was she? And why had she vanished after ridding him of the Devil's grandson and his accomplice?

As these thoughts went through his head, out of the distance came a prolonged, resonant wail: "Come back, my precious joy!"

It was Yolanda. She was calling him. Their cursed neighbours had managed to awake her with their cries.

"Come back, my precious soul," she said, and her voice rose upon the air, bounced off the ceiling, lingered among the piles of boxes like an echo. "Come back, my heart. Don't leave me with only buttons to play with."

He should not call back; that would reveal his hiding place. But how could he go on with his dream knowing that his wife was worrying herself sick?

"I won't leave you, my love," he said. "Go back to sleep."

Then he peered over the edge again.

On the floor below men were standing with their necks craned, looking up at him.

The only way he could escape them was to fly away. But he did not fly in his dreams anymore. Should he call Zephira to his rescue? But what would she think of him, seeing how impotent he was once again? A gloomy rage swelled in him. Why was he so helpless while everyone else seemed all-powerful? Had it always been like that in his dreams? Had he always been this helpless and considerate, while everyone else was all-powerful and devoid of scruples? Definitely, this was not the usual vision of the land of dreams: a place where people are supposed to live as glorified images of themselves.

Suddenly the box he was perched on started to tilt back and forth, threatening to throw him crashing headlong down onto the floor. Holding tight to it, he peered over the edge once more as the void dipped and swooped around him.

The men were crawling up the steep bank of the boxes after their quarry, their teeth bared and their eyes giddy with the anticipation of flesh and blood.

I'm done, he thought.

Right then a hand shot out from a hole in the ceiling above, grabbed him by the hair, and pulled him off the box.

14

YOLANDA TOO HAD a dream before she awoke again, later that night. But Lukas was not in her dream. In her dream, Yolanda was with Daniel Bouchard. The two were in Vienna, a city Yolanda had visited with her sister one summer, on a tour of Europe, when they were still in college. Yolanda and Daniel were in evening dress, going down a sumptuous alley lined with statues of Greek gods and goddesses, nymphs and satyrs, towards the brightly lit facade of an opera house. Only Daniel was walking. With one arm round Yolanda's waist, he was holding her up, two inches above the ground, because in Vienna, he said, the feet of a fiancée must never touch the pavement.

Daniel's mother was following behind. She was furious. Her husband had never held her up, her feet always touched the ground. Indeed, she was so incensed that she could not restrain her rage and she exploded, literally. Yolanda was glad to be rid of her. But Daniel could not leave his mother scattered all over the cobblestones, at the mercy of the tires of every passing limousine. They should pick up the pieces and place them on the curb, he said. Yolanda looked at the hundreds of body parts strewn around her like the pieces of a puzzle and woke up.

Lukas was not lying in bed, next to her. She switched on the bedside lamp and looked at the alarm clock. It was 3:10 A.M.

She called out her husband's name, but she got no reply.

"Lukas," she called out again. "Where are you? What are you doing?"

Again there was no reply. She left her bed and, fuzzy still from sleep, she dragged herself to the bathroom. Lukas always took a shower when he came home from work, but the floor under the shower was dry.

Yolanda went down to the first floor. There was no light there either, nor any sign of her husband. Yet she was sure she had heard the garage door open and close before she dozed off. Could it have been Voula, the forty-five-year-old spinster who lived in their basement flat? The emergency exit of her flat led to the two-car garage. But why would Voula open and close its door in the middle of the night? Her car was always parked outside.

Yolanda opened the door leading down to the garage.

"Lukas? Are you down there?"

This time she waited less than a heartbeat for a reply. As soon as she breathed in again, after her last word, she smelled the strong fumes of auto exhaust and rushed down the five steps that led to the garage. And for a moment, standing on the last step, she thought she was surfacing from one dream, into another.

Lukas's car was there, next to hers. The door on the driver's side was open. The garage door was wide open as well. And there, in the opening, under the light above the garage door which Lukas had left on, Yolanda's husband lay on his back on the cement floor. Kneeling next to him in her dressing gown, Voula was hunched over his face and was kissing his mouth.

Yolanda was only wearing a nightshirt. But it took her more than one heartbeat before she reacted to the arctic air blowing through the garage door and realized that her husband had not opened it to have a better view of the night sky as his tenant kissed his lips, that Voula was giving him mouth-to-mouth resuscitation, breathing for him at the rate of one breath every three seconds.

"What's going on? What happened?"

She never got a reply from Voula either. An ambulance had pulled up in front of the garage and two paramedics jumped out. She never remembered how she got into her coat and boots. She only recalled coming down again and hearing one of the paramedics say on the ambulance radio: "Pupils unresponsive. No response to pain either, extensor or otherwise." Then the other paramedic helped her climb into the ambulance through its rear door and told her to sit next to the stretcher on which Lukas now lay and fasten her seat belt. She later remembered Voula, her eyes watering, saying to the paramedic, as the reflection of the ambulance's red light bounced off her face: "I'm the one who saved him! And I'm a registered nurse!"

The paramedic shot back: "There's only room for his wife!" Then he shut the rear door of the vehicle and got into the passenger seat. The ambulance roared away through deserted streets, its pedal driven hard to the floorboard and its siren wailing at every intersection, a wild electronic whoop ascending through cycles in the cold and silent February night.

It all happened so quickly after she woke from her Vienna dream — and she had seen so many similar scenes on television — that it took a while for reality to sink in. Maybe her mind rejected that reality because of the hint of guilt it was laced with: if she had not fallen asleep, Lukas would be in bed now. Whatever, when the ambulance turned south on Park Avenue towards Mount Royal, she took refuge in the immutability of the past and let her thoughts take her back to the Café Acropole, a night club that had stood at that corner until the late 1970s.

A distant cousin, who had recently immigrated to Montreal, had asked her to accompany him there, to a wedding reception. The groom was the owner of the restaurant where her cousin and Lukas worked. By the end of the evening, Yolanda and Lukas had met and danced together, then each went home to relive those moments. By the time they celebrated their own wedding, the cousin had moved to Chicago and Yolanda never heard from him again. She never gave him a moment's thought either after he moved away. And now, as she sat ramrod straight, gazing at her husband's handsome face half-covered by an an oxygen mask, she thought of that cousin and the role some people play in our lives, appearing in them for a brief moment, to set them on a new course, then vanishing again.

When the ambulance sped by the mountain, the few cars on the road pulling over to let it pass, Yolanda sank once again into the past, to the first time she walked on that mountain with Lukas. She was working weekends at Eaton's as a salesgirl, and he had come to fetch her that Friday night after she finished work at nine, and walk her home. It was early June, the night sky was clear and full of stars and promises, the air was warmer than it had been in months and fragrant with the heady smells of apple trees in bloom and lilacs and freshly mowed grass. They sat on a bench, and soon they were kissing. And they went on kissing until two uniformed police officers aimed their flashlights at their faces and told them to move on. It was forbidden to loiter in a public park at night, after eleven o'clock.

"Our first kiss lasted two hours," she finally whispered. "You remember?"

The only thing that moved on Lukas's face was the intermittent flashing glare of the street lights rushing by.

Maybe he had not heard, she thought, what with the roar of the siren and the crackle of the ambulance two-way radio. So she squeezed his hand, leaned her face closer to his, and, in a lighter tone, she whispered again, this time in his ear:

"Finally, Voula got her wish. She kissed you on the mouth."

Again she watched his face for a sign of life, focusing this time on the laugh lines around his eyes.

Nothing.

15

AS SURE AS Lukas was of his eyes when they saw Zephira grab the Bug Buster, so was he sure that hers was the hand pulling him through that hole. Yet, when he emerged on the other side, there was no one there. Only rows upon rows of graves that stretched out as far as he could see.

He thought: Like her expeditious disposal of Nestor and Elaine, Zephira's flight into the warehouse was an unequivocal confirmation of her desire to see me, since it has led me to the cemetery. But why has she vanished again?

It was a radiant morning. The white marble tombs glittered under the sun, the earth between them was carpeted with poppies and daisies, and the air was filled with swallows executing their annual spring dance. Lukas had not seen a swallow in many years, and their flight filled him with hope. These harbingers of fair weather could only be a good omen.

Ablaze with new hope, he searched for Zephira's grave.

Aside from the names of their occupants, their dates of birth and death, the graves also bore an epitaph or an inscription. "Journey's End Hotel," one said. "Death is not the worst thing there is," another said. "Don't forget me," most of them said to the relatives and friends who came to wash and scrub the grave, light the oil candle, or pay their respects. Some also bore signs pointing to stacks of pictures of the deceased. "Please take one," they said.

Some visitors had brought picnic baskets. Before every sip of wine they poured a few drops from their glasses over the grave on which they had spread an assortment of food.

"How hungry he must be for a tomato salad and fried calamari," a woman said.

A man took the lit cigarette out of his mouth and planted it filter downward in the earth so that the departed could enjoy a smoke as he must have enjoyed it while he was alive.

Many tombs were also adorned with a photograph of the deceased behind glass. One had a small video screen. The tape was a few seconds long and showed over and over a hockey player scoring a goal. A middle-aged woman was sitting next to the grave, in a folding chair. Standing before her, was a minister begging her to go home. Lukas wanted to ask them if they knew the location of Zephira's grave, but the woman would not stop talking.

"I won't move," she said. "Not until you've moved my husband's two new neighbours elsewhere. What an idea — burying these two next to him. Who is this Inge on his right and this Margarita on his left, anyway? I'm sure they've never seen a hockey game. And look at their ages. Nineteen. Twenty-two. What could my husband talk to them about? They have nothing in common. No, no. I won't budge until you've moved these two elsewhere."

"We can't move them," the minister said, "without the consent of their families, and they won't give it."

"Move my husband. I give you my consent. So long as you move him among men. A man needs to be among other men, much as every living thing needs to be among its own kind."

"Madam, your husband is no longer a man."

"How do you know?"

Obviously, they were not about to stop arguing, so Lukas hurried away.

He stopped again at a souvenir stand run by a young nun. Yolanda might not be as jealous and possessive as the hockey player's wife, and he was grateful for that, still she would ask him what he was doing at Eaton's. Fortunately, the nun sold candles. Yolanda loved candles.

"You light them to the accompaniment of these incantations," the nun explained, showing Lukas a sheet of paper. "They're designed to placate spirits that will roam the earth if they're not appeased."

Lukas bought two candles. One for Yolanda and one for himself, to use in case he awakened before finding Zephira, to placate her until his next trip.

"How about a rope of a suicide?" the nun said. "Maybe a

piece of the gauze Lazarus was wrapped in? They're certified, every one of them."

"No, thank you," Lukas said as he paid. "I'd like some information, though. I'm looking for the grave of Zephira from Leros. She was the daughter of Anestis the fisherman."

"I don't know the location of each grave. I know, however, that the Leros section is down this alley, past the blue gate."

Lukas put the candles and the sheet of incantations in his pocket and headed towards the blue gate. Now he was sure at least to find Zephira's father. He would know where his daughter was buried.

Men bowed as he passed. Women smiled at him. On his left, a black-clad Hasidic brass band was playing "Sentimental Journey" around a tomb. On his right, a man was delivering a funeral sermon. "I must confess," he was saying, "that it is a pleasure to bury such people as this brother of mine."

Further down Lukas came upon Claude, a young actor who had worked at his restaurant until he had made himself a name as a playwright with a monologue entitled *Condemned to Life*. He was standing slumped, staring into an open grave. There was no coffin in the grave, no priest, no mourners, no one except himself. Was he gathering material for his next play?

"No," Claude said. "I'm contemplating moving here."

Now Lukas was in a hurry — he had to find Anestis, then Zephira, then help Aris unearth Artemis's temple. But he could not bear the notion of a young man moving into a grave so early in life. So he said: "The critics loved your play.

You got a grant to write another. Why would you want to move here, and on such a beautiful day?"

"You know damn well why."

"Because I didn't like your play? What do I know about the theatre?"

"Then on what grounds did you judge my work?"

"I was bored. So much gloom. You talk of life as if it were a disease. Why? You're young, in good health. You have a dream, a cheerful disposition — otherwise I'd never have hired you as a waiter —"

"You can't do that!"

"What?"

"Confuse the artist with his creation. They are two separate things. Furthermore, the function of a play is to elevate the mind, not fill the belly. And you can elevate the mind only by depressing it."

"You should have told me. How was I supposed to know? My only education has been life's hardships and little everyday miracles."

Claude rolled his eyes. "Please! Not that drivel again about how a woman has only to smile to you and you see life beckoning you again, full of delights and possibilities!"

Piqued, Lukas felt like shoving Claude into the grave himself. Instead he said: "I have other examples. I'll tell you about them when I get back. I won't be long."

Then he rushed away.

Suddenly a man grabbed his arm. "Help me," he said. "This can't go on."

He pointed to a woman kneeling beside a grave, smearing mud on her face and all over her head. On the grave was a picture of a fifteen-year-old boy.

"Every morning she comes. Talk to her. She thinks I'm heartless. How could I be? He was my son too. Please talk to her. I don't know what to say anymore."

Now Lukas was in more of a hurry: he had to find Anestis and Zephira, then help Aris, and come back to convince Claude to go back to his life. So he pushed the man away. Even if he wanted to get involved, what could he possibly tell a mother who had lost her fifteen-year-old son?

"Dreams," he suddenly said.

"Dreams?"

"You can unite them again through dreams. Call Judy Yamada. She'll explain everything."

16

A TRUCK LOADED with pine boxes brought for burial was going through the blue gate. The gate was low and some of the boxes were knocked off the top and fell to the ground, scattering their contents. The driver got off the truck to pick them up, while women rushed forward, touched the corpses, then rushed back and touched the children accompanying them.

Lukas asked the driver if he knew where Anestis the fisherman was buried.

The truck driver replied: "Go straight ahead, up that rise, then down the other side."

Lukas went straight ahead, up the rise, then down the other side, and came upon a dump site filled with a jumble of rotting caskets and wooden crates mixed with a scattering of moss-covered bones and skulls, old tires, rusty auto parts and other junk. There were no wreaths here, no flowers, no visitors — only rats the size of cats. When he finally found the crate with Anestis's name on it, he opened the lid to look inside. The interior reeked of mildew; deep inside it, as if he were looking down a well, he saw the old fisherman sitting cross-legged at the bottom, dealing himself a game of solitaire.

"What a sad resting place for a man who spent his life riding the waves," Lukas whispered to himself.

The old fisherman looked up, as if he had heard him.

"May your bones end up at the bottom of a cesspool," he said. "If it weren't for you, my daughter would have stayed in Leros and given me a proper grave for people to visit and remember me by; may you and your name be forever forgotten in the hearts and minds of men. But my pride and joy left the island. Because not one of you sons of bitches would marry a girl with no dowry, may all your daughters marry a pimp. How could I give her a dowry, you bastard, when everyone paid so little for my fish; may you spend eternity chewing your entrails."

Then he went back to his game of solitaire, cursing the men of Leros and spitting at every other word, as if his lips were still covered with salt.

Lukas lowered his head in shame. Not only had he hurt Zephira, he had also condemned her father to spend eternity in a dump. No wonder she would not spare a glance for him.

"I'll make it up to you, Anestis," he said. "I'll have you moved to a new grave."

The dead fisherman looked up again. Lukas showed him his wallet stuffed full of banknotes and credit cards.

"Could you tell me where Zephira is buried," he said. "I want to check her accommodations too."

"Have me moved out of here first," Anestis replied.

17

HE CLIMBED UP the rise again, taking great care not to touch any caskets or crates and awaken other unpleasant memories. He thought all the while: Now I have to find Zephira, help Aris, convince Claude to go back to his life, and get Anestis moved to a new grave. Where will I find the time to do all this? And where should I start? Surely with the cemetery's superintendent. Only he can give Anestis a proper grave and direct me to Zephira's. He might even sell me a shovel, to replace the one I've lost.

He looked around for someone to direct him to the superintendent's office, and saw a man sitting on a chair, in front of his grave.

Lukas felt his throat tighten. The man was his own father. And he had seen him too, and was slowly rising to his feet.

Now Lukas could not tell his father that he was looking for the superintendent to obtain from him the location of Zephira's grave. His father would be hurt to learn that he had not come for him. Worse: he would tell his wife, and once again she would try to stop her son from talking to the girl. And that upset Lukas very much — to be fifty-eight years old and still unable to discuss those things closest to his heart with his father. But he hid his feelings. This was no time to rekindle old quarrels.

So he cleared his throat and said: "Finally, I found you."

His father smiled. "Did you drop by your mother's grave?"

"Not yet."

"She'll be very happy to see you. Even if you never offer her a memorial service, she still loves you like a mother should love her child."

Lukas, who was not a church-going man, had never offered his father a memorial service either. But his father was too proud to complain about that. He only said: "If I had a mother like yours, I would visit her every day. But I had no mother. No father either. And because I had no mother and no father, as far as I can remember, I had to work or starve. But I've learned a few things. And what I've learned I shall teach you to make sure you never go hungry."

He pulled a wooden crate out of his grave. The crate was filled with fish neatly laid out on a bed of moth balls. His father picked one up and said: "The most important thing about fish is freshness. The signs of freshness are five."

Lukas had so many things to do and so little time left. He

wanted to tell his father that he knew all there was to know about fish, that he had done well for himself and would never go hungry, but his old man was so happy to see him and so eager to offer him what little he possessed that he did not have the heart to interrupt him.

"One: the fresh fish does not smell of fish; it has the mild, briny smell of the sea. Two: its flesh is elastic and firm to the touch. Three: the eyes —"

Suddenly, an idea occurred to Lukas. He said: "Have you found your parents?"

His father stared at the eyes of the dead fish in the same way they stared back at him, and shook his head no.

"You should put out an ad," his son said.

"I did. Now I don't dare take a walk, in case whoever my mother or father was comes by while I'm away."

He cleared his throat, as he had always cleared it when he held back his emotions, then went on to say: "You don't know how lucky you are to have a mother like yours. I know, I shouldn't judge. Some women have their reasons for abandoning a child. But in death? What reasons could they have in death?"

He straightened his back. "Don't forget to drop by your mother's grave. She's a good woman. I like to see her happy. And she's happiest when you think of her."

He looked at the fish again. "Where was I? Yes, the eyes. The eyes of a fresh fish —"

"Have you asked the superintendent about your parents?"

"He's a hard man to get hold of. All those dead —"

He probably wanted money and his father was too proud to say that he did not have enough to grease his palm.

"I'll talk to him."

His father suppressed a smile. "You will?"

"Yes. Where can I find him?"

"At the rally. That's where he is today. It's that way, sixteen thousand graves from here."

He cleared his throat again.

"You will be back — this time? To tell me how it went."

Lukas wanted to reassure him and soothe him with a hug, but his father might deduce from the hug that he did not intend to come back this time either. He would hug him after his meeting with Zephira. He would return then to take his father out for the cup of coffee he never had the opportunity to buy him when he was alive. While they drank their coffee, he would tell the man whom for years he tried so hard not to resemble how — in the way he now carried himself, in the way he cleared his throat, in the way he raised his left eyebrow when his gaze bore down on others, even in the way he smiled and danced — he saw every day a perfect imitation of his old man. Surely his father would be happy to hear that.

"I'll be back," he said. "But don't tell my mother. I want to surprise her."

18

HE WALKED AWAY, dazed and forlorn among the graves.

"Sixteen thousand graves! I'll never reach that rally before I wake."

Suddenly Aris appeared before him, holding his shovel.

"What's going on?" he said. "Where have you been? Where is the shovel I gave you?"

Lukas told him how he had been bumping into people to whom he had never given a moment's thought, while he could not find the girl who had occupied his thoughts for the better part of his life. He also told him of the new wrongs he had to atone for, the new responsibilities he had taken on.

"I could look for my father's parents in another dream," he concluded. "But Zephira won't give me another chance, and I'll spend the rest of my life seeing me abandon her on that shore, without the slightest hope of redemption."

"Maybe that's what she wants."

"If it weren't for her, I'd still be running after Nestor. That in itself would have been the cruelest punishment."

"Where is she then? Why does she keep eluding you?"

"She has her pride. I've left her in the lurch three times; it's only proper that I go to her grave to offer my apologies."

It was the first time he was mentioned his one moment of cowardice to anyone. There was such despair in his voice that Aris took pity on him.

"I'll fly you to the rally," he said.

That boosted Lukas's hopes and renewed his resolve. He promised the best friend he ever had to find a shovel and, in turn, help him unearth Artemis's temple. Then he held tightly onto Aris's belt, and they flew off over the Leros section of the cemetery with its crazy-quilt of graves strewn over a treeless landscape laced by an elaborate system of stairs and paths.

Filled with the twinge of anguish and exhilaration that accompanied every flight, for a moment Lukas forgot Zephira and all the dead that lay across the surface of the earth. But word had spread that he was on his way to see the superintendent, and those dissatisfied with the accommodation of their graves begged him to intervene on their behalf, their voices wafted from below to his ears by the wind. Only once did he ask Aris to slow down. He had heard a familiar voice, and when Aris lurched to the left and glided back to circle over an upscale section of tombs and mausoleums spread out over flat and well-manicured lawns, Lukas recognized one of his former customers.

"I designed some of the better known buildings in Montreal and Canada," the man said. "I taught and trained hundreds of young architects. I sat on the boards of the Red Cross and Amnesty International and the Montreal Symphony Orchestra. I wrote three books and sailed round the globe two times. What photograph did my children put on my grave? The only photograph of me carving a turkey. Tell them to change it when you get back home."

Lukas promised he would talk to his children, then the two friends flew away and soon they spotted a huge crowd. Although Lukas was happy that he was finally to know the location of Zephira's grave, he could not help but feel a tinge of sadness at the flight ending so quickly. As they descended, he prayed that after he found his joy again, he would be able to fly at least one more time on his own before he too was put away in a grave.

19

FROM ATOP A rock, a man was addressing a gathering led by a group of priests and officials. Lukas pushed his way through the crowd towards them and asked to speak to the superintendent. Like the priests and the other officials, the superintendent was so enthralled by the speech that he told him to wait till it was over.

The speaker was young and handsome, yet he cut a venerable figure with his tall frame wrapped round in a cloak, his beard and his flowing hair. He addressed the crowd with dramatic gestures and his strong voice carried to the whole of the attendance.

"As you hear my voice, I heard the voice say: 'Write in that book the things which you have seen, and the things which are, and the things which shall take place after these things.'"

Aris asked the woman next to him who the speaker was.

"The apostle John," she replied. "He's looking for a quiet island on which to settle and write a book that will make the island that takes him in famous. I would gladly put him up at my place. Imagine — a writer! And so handsomely divine."

"Then," John went on, "the voice said: 'Write also in that book that they should give up their idols and their books, for he who wants to increase his knowledge increases his sorrow.'"

Boisterous cheering rose from the ranks of clerics and a group of teenagers.

Aris said to Lukas: "Did you hear that crap? If that guy settles here, he'll never let us unearth Artemis's temple. We must chase him away."

"After I talk to the superintendent."

"It might be too late. Let me climb on your shoulders so I can be heard. I only need to say two words."

He handed Lukas his shovel, then climbed onto his shoulders.

"Lastly," John was saying now, "the voice said: 'Tell all those who are dead and thirsty for redemption to be faithful only to the ruler of the keys of Hades, and they shall thirst no more, neither shall they ever be forgotten by the living.'"

That pleased the crowd a lot, that all their past sins would be forgiven and their names forever etched in the hearts of the living. It cheered the speaker, and one of the women cheering the loudest was Zephira herself. She was standing a few feet away from Lukas. But he could not call out her name; the cheering was too loud. He could not walk up to her either; he was nailed to the spot by his friend's weight.

So he dropped the shovel and waved his hands, to get her attention.

Meanwhile, the cheering subsided and Aris began speaking from atop his friend to the crowd: "All writers hear voices. All writers claim that their book will make their island famous. All writers wish that their book is the only one people will read. This writer, however, is the first one who has the gall to ask openly for the destruction of all other books. Is it really because they increase your sorrow, or is it because they might tell you that no one can forgive us our sins because we create our own heavens and our own hells? That the voice this man claims to have heard is only a product of his fancy, to secure himself eternal life in the hearts of men, because unlike his idol, he can't pull off the resurrection con?"

"Blasphemy!" cried the priests, sprinkling holy water at Aris to chase the evil spirit in him.

Lukas, his body collapsing under Aris's weight, pleaded with him to shut up and get off his shoulders so he could run to Zephira; but in vain.

"I too had a revelation," he continued, raising his voice above the din. "After you've burnt your books, I saw you grovel on your knees, your bodies covered with heavy garments so that your nakedness would not be revealed; your minds clothed with this man's Oriental superstitions; your hearts filled, not with love and curiosity towards all things, but with premonitions of deluge, pestilence, fire and brimstone."

"How could such a handsome young man be ashamed

of his body?" said the woman next to him. "Surely you're stretching it a bit."

"Ask him. If he's honest, he'll tell you. He'll embrace you if you slaughter thousands, to defend his book; and condemn you to eternal fire if you so much as masturbate."

A grumble rose from a group of teenage boys.

John raised his eyes to the sky. "Is that how it will be?"

As the apostle listened silently for the voice he alone could hear, Lukas turned again towards Zephira, but she had vanished once more.

Finally, John said: "The voice said: 'He who keeps My deeds until the end, to him will I give authority over the nations, and he shall rule them till the end of time.'"

A chorus of hallelujahs erupted from the group of stiff-faced representatives of the government and of the army.

"Oh, Lord," said a general whose chest gleamed with medals and heavily ornamented ribbons, "thank You for sending us a Yoannis to guide us and march at our side."

And, together with the clergymen, the superintendent and the other officials, and surrounded by security police in dark suits and tinted sunglasses, he meandered through the crowd and towards the orator, as the sounds of a military band filled the air and the people lavished applause upon their new hero and chanted, "Yo-a-nnis! Yo-a-nnis!"

Sensing that he had lost the battle, Aris made a last attempt to win the war. He jumped off Lukas's shoulders, and, having realized that if you can get people to believe in a certain heaven, you can get them to believe in anything, he told the teenage boys: "In my revelation I saw you go to ninth heaven, each with seventy-two virgins, if you help that stranger discover the pleasures of the flesh. If not, behold, he'll soon cast you upon a bed of impotency and a life of singing Hare Krishna in airports."

At their age, the image of seventy-two virgins sufficed to summon an erection as big and hard as befitted the boys' youth. Armed with it, they pushed towards John, crying: "Hurrah for ninth heaven!"

Upon seeing what they intended to attack him with, John turned on his heels and ran for his chastity, the boys running after him so fast no one could stop them.

But some merchants did manage to corner Aris. They said to him: "You jerk. Every island has something to attract tourists, except ours. His book would have brought them in droves, and all of us would have profited, including you."

"I'll make you famous," Aris said. "My friend Lukas has returned from Canada, and by nightfall we will have found the temple of Artemis."

"How?" they said. "You don't even have a shovel!"

"Sure we do," Aris said, turning to his friend.

Lukas looked down at his feet: the shovel was gone.

"It was right here," he said, checking the people around him, but no one was carrying a shovel.

In vain Aris tried to reassure the merchants that he would find it; they refused to let him go.

"Let your Canadian friend look for it," they said. "We shall keep you hostage until he does."

Aris said to Lukas: "Do me a favour. If you don't find the shovel, check to make sure I'm not breathing first before anybody takes the liberty of putting me in the ground."

Lukas started looking for the shovel, convinced that it had been taken by the priests. Since that rat Nestor could no longer stop him himself, he probably used his father's connections to delay him, knowing that he would not search for Zephira until he had found a shovel and saved his friend.

Unless he could convince John to come back. That might annoy Aris, but it would certainly please the superintendent. So much that he might grant him all his wishes for free.

He searched with his eyes for John. The apostle had reached the shore. As the boys were about to catch him, he threw his cloak on the waves, and, using it as a raft, he floated away, crying back at his pursuers: "Scum! God's curse be upon you and your adulterated island!"

When Lukas reached the shore, the boys were gone. He cupped his hands round his mouth and called out: "Please come back. I'm thirsty for redemption."

John cupped his hands round his ears as if he could not hear what Lukas was saying.

Lukas had to get closer to him. But at his age, not only could he not fly, he could no longer swim that far either.

He looked around for a boat he could use.

20

THERE WAS NO boat anywhere. There was, however, a fountain. Lukas cupped his hands under the tap and, in sips, he drank the water flowing into them. But no matter how quickly and thirstily he drank at the small pool inside his hands, most of the water ran through his fingers, down to the ground and back to the sea. So he glued his lips round the tap and sucked, never taking a breath, until the flow of water petered out into a trickle, and the trickle into dew. He banged on the tap, to make sure no water was left. The tap gargled and small shellfish fell out, along with little crabs and sand and everything the sea contained — aside from water — that was small enough to pass through the opening.

He turned to the sea: it was emptied of all its water and John was standing on its exposed bed. But Lukas could not go to him. Another sea surrounded him now. A sea of ravenous, mangy packs of cats. Some were scratching the earth with their claws, in search of water. Others, crouched low, glaring at him, showing their teeth.

"Lukas!" a voice called. "We have no water!"

It was Xavier, his previous tenant. He was standing between the sea of thirsty cats and the sea emptied of its water.

"Call the city," Lukas replied.

"I did. It's not the city that cut the water off. You should call a plumber."

"You call him. I'm busy right now."

As Lukas said the last word, a cat leapt up and, hanging with its claws onto his shirt, pushed its head into his mouth, looking for water all the way to his tonsils.

Lukas felt his entrails rise to his throat, and he retched in uncontrollable spasms. Now dozens of cats jumped at him, clawing and fighting their way to his mouth, to lap up the liquid pouring from it, when an old gypsy woman appeared, covered with a large wrap and holding a shovel. She chased the cats with it, led Lukas into the shade of some trees, wiped off his mouth and chin, waited for him to get his breath back, then said: "I heard you were looking for a shovel."

Lukas said: "Not only have you saved me from certain death, you've saved my best friend's life as well."

He gave her twice the amount she was asking. He also gave her his business card. "Drop by my restaurant when you visit Montreal. I'll throw you the biggest party you've ever seen."

Holding the shovel tightly in his hand, he looked for the way back to the rally, but in whatever direction he turned he saw only trees. He looked for the gypsy, but she had vanished.

"Lukas," his former tenant was calling again, "the plumber won't fix the problem unless you give him the okay."

"I can't talk to him! Tell him to call my wife!"

"She's busy calling an ambulance for you."

"Jesus."

"What do I do? I need to take a shower."

"Pay the plumber, then deduct the sum from next month's rent."

"Whatever the cost?"

"Whatever the cost. And tell my wife to send the ambulance back. I only took a sleeping pill. I'll wake by myself when I'm through here."

He moved on, his ears scanning the silence for sounds of the rally. Instead he heard swift steps behind him. He stopped.

The footfalls stopped.

He looked back: there was no one.

"Xavier, is that you again?"

Silence.

"Apostle John?"

Silence.

"Maybe I heard wrong. Maybe those weren't footfalls at all."

He moved on. Swift steps were following him again. And again he stopped. The footfalls stopped too.

"Who's that? Show your face. Who's following me?"

He waited for a reply, but received only silence.

He moved on. The footfalls echoed behind him again. So he stopped once more, alert to everything that moved. The stillness was everywhere.

"Damn woods. Always crawling with all sorts of life, except human. Like a tomb. No wonder they always had a strange effect on me."

He hurried on, changing directions to lose his pursuer, moving stealthily from the cover of one tree to another, his steps leading him into thicker and darker woods which closed in on him like the jaws of death, and when he heard his stalker's footsteps again, he thought that he had not only lost his way but that he was about to lose his wits as well.

He gave a desperate cry: "Who are you? What do you want from me?"

He strained his ears, attentive to any sound not native to the woods. This time, in the stillness, he heard a click. Then another click. And another.

The ticking of a clock? Whatever it was, it was close to him. Very close. Indeed, it came from the shovel he was holding. He put his ear against it: the ticking came from inside the handle. The ticking of a bomb? Why would the gypsy plant a bomb in the shovel? Could she be working for the Devil's grandson? Could this be another one of that rat's delay tactics? If so, why did the gypsy save him from the cats?

He unscrewed the handle: it was as hollow as a straw and as empty. Yet the ticking continued, like a funeral march, and, for sure, it was coming from inside the handle.

He grunted: a grunt of frustration, with a touch of panic. "Where is the damn bomb!"

Suddenly there was a tick louder than the previous ones. He dropped the handle, and was about to take to his heels, when a tremendous explosion hurled him to the ground, face down.

When the stillness settled again, he lifted his head and found himself lying at the edge of a hole as large as a grave and so deep he could not see the bottom.

Slowly he tottered to his feet. But no sooner had he stood up than the gypsy woman reappeared, looking much taller now. She hurled herself against him and pushed him with all her weight and strength over the edge.

Hanging now by his fingernails over the bottomless grave and searching for a foothold below, Lukas looked up at the woman and said: "Why?"

She pulled away the large gypsy wrap covering half her face, so Lukas could see who she was: Zephira's mother.

"I want you buried next to me," she said, "so I can torture you for all eternity."

Lukas wanted to tell her how sorry he was for the suffering he might have caused her daughter and her husband and her, that he had come to make up for it, but the woman stepped on his fingers and hammered them with her heels. The pain that shot through his arm and into his entire body was so violent that he was about to let go of the edge and fall into that blackness, when he heard another voice — a girl's voice — say: "Mother! Let him be!"

The woman stopped and looked down at Lukas. "May your child suffer as mine has suffered!" she spat into his face, then she was gone.

When Lukas hauled himself out of the hole and back onto the ground again, all he saw was a shadow, with Zephira's crown of hair, scuttling into the trees and vanishing.

21

LUKAS RAN IN the direction of the shadow and saw a glade shining like an oasis of light in that dark labyrinth of trees. As he moved towards it, he came upon the Radar.

"What are you doing out, at this hour?" said his old primary school teacher, blocking his way. "It is the hour when the sun is highest and the crickets loudest. Have you forgotten that lesson as well? It is the hour when the midday demons appear in the shape of beautiful girls to beguile the wandering into dancing with them till they go mad. Go home. Even grown men retreat at this hour to the safety of blessed slumber."

Lukas had grown bigger and stronger than his old teacher. He could easily shove him aside. Instead, he said: "What are *you* doing out, at this hour?"

"How dare you!" the Radar roared. And he stooped to pick up something to whip his old pupil with.

Lukas scooted off, and stepped out of the shade and into the light.

He stopped again, blinded now by the dazzling brilliance of the steamy reflections of the glaring sun on the shimmering surface of the earth. He shaded his eyes with the palm of his hand, and saw a human shape — a mere silhouette — come out of the haze, towards him, white veils flowing from it and heat waves swimming up around it.

"Come," said a girl's pleasant voice.

A hand slipped into the crook of his arm. It guided him to the centre of the glade. There the midday heat was so intense that he could hardly breathe, only gasp, when he said: "I've finally found you."

"Sit down."

He sat on the ground. The female shape took some cool water from a brook in her cupped hands and poured it over his eyes, washing away the veil of haze. Now Lukas could see again. But instead of Zephira, he saw Penny, one of his daughter's best friends. He looked around. The glade was filled with girls and young women, all of them friends and acquaintances, past and present, of his daughter. Some, like Penny, were wearing white robes, almond blossoms in their hair, and little bells round their ankles. Others, like Linda, whom Lukas had known since she was six, were bathing naked in the brook, or sitting on its banks, combing each other, like regular water nymphs. They were so ravishing and enchanting that Lukas forgot all he had been through since he embarked on his dream.

"Thank you, Penny," he said, glad to be back with the living again, if only for a moment. "You've refreshed my heart as well as my eyes."

"What would you like?" Penny said. "You may ask anything your soul desires. It's our turn to wait on you, to thank you for all the beautiful evenings we've spent at your restaurant."

"I want to speak to Zephira. Where is she? I saw her enter this glade."

A woman whom Lukas had seen only once said: "She stopped to freshen up, and went back to her grave."

"Why? She wants to see me, otherwise she wouldn't have saved me so many times. Yet she vanishes every time."

"She has her pride too," the woman said. "If the roles were reversed, wouldn't you expect her to call on you at your grave and make your apologies there?"

Lukas smiled. He had guessed right and Aris had guessed wrong.

"Where is her grave?" he said.

"On a seashore like the one where you two last saw the little waves carry the full moon to your feet."

Lukas was moved to tears when he heard where Zephira had chosen to spend her death.

"Tell her I'll go to her after I free Aris," he said. "Would you have a shovel by any chance?"

"Dance with us first, and we'll give you two," said Linda, her naked body wet and dripping with water.

"Dance, dance, dance," the others chanted, forming a circle around him. Then, swinging to and fro, clapping their hands and thumping their feet, the little bells tied round their ankles filling the air with their tinkling, they sang an old song Lukas's mother used to sing back when he used to ride his tricycle faster than the wind:

First kiss is "How are you?"

"Have pity on me," Lukas said. "Even if I had the time, I couldn't, at my age and in this heat, dance with every one of you."

"You're a betting man. Find a way to improve your odds," Monique, Irene's law partner, said, while Linda, her body glistening under the scorching sun, shook her breasts and belly and thighs at him like a belly-dancer, as the others sang:

Second kiss is "I like you."
Only if you give me three,
I'll know that you love me.

"Could we have a bite first," Lukas said, hoping food would weigh down their bodies and dull their senses, and they would be less inclined to such frolic. "I haven't eaten since I left home."

The girls rushed to the brook where eels slithered by in the clear and shallow water, or stood immobile, their mouths glued onto a rock as if they were sucking it. Giggling and laughing, they fished them out with their bare hands and dropped them at Lukas's feet. Some brought baskets filled with glasses and an assortment of wines. They offered Lukas a glass, they filled theirs, and when the fish stopped struggling for air, each picked one and nibbled on it as they had seen Lukas eat his favourite fish — fried sardines — holding them by each end, like corn on the cob.

The older he got, the prettier and younger they looked. Damn brain, he thought, as his eyes roved from sensuous figure to sensuous figure. It can comprehend and concede anything, from the Big Bang to the existence of black holes it has never seen, yet it can't admit and resign itself to the most obvious — the aging of the body that houses it.

"Stop sighing," the girls said. "You said you were hungry. Eat. Otherwise the fish will go to waste, and that would be a pity," they added, mimicking his accent and throaty voice.

"Give him some bread," Penny said. "He can't eat without bread."

They gave him bread, and Linda pinned almond blossoms on his mane of silvery-white undulating locks, saying all the while: "I love you."

"I love you too, sweetheart."

"But I really love you. I've always loved you."

"I've always loved you too — like a daughter."

"But I'm not your daughter."

Her lips were swolen with desire and her gaze was seeking out his own with such intensity that Lukas felt his penis harden as it had not hardened in a long while. Though he wanted to feel that hardness of a bygone youth a bit longer, he looked away. But wherever he settled his eyes there was a body in glorious full bloom to fill his brainless lower head with foolish notions. Lest the girls notice it and tell his daughter, he bent his chest over to hide it.

"What's the matter?" Penny asked.

"The sun is too bright for my eyes," he said, his forehead almost touching the ground.

Penny lifted her robe and passed it over his head, covering it. "How's that? Can you see your fish now?"

He raised his eyes and saw a triangle of white cotton, only a tongue's length away.

I should have heeded the Radar's warning, he groaned, both his heads swarming now with thoughts so irreverent that they bordered in his mind on incest. I better leave this place before I lose every desire to go back to the dead.

Just then a cry was heard in the distance: "You bastard! How could you!"

He pulled his head out from under the robe, scrambled to his feet, and saw his daughter vanish in the thicket, while more faintly now came the words:

"You bastard! With my friends!"

22

HE WAS RUNNING once again, this time after his daughter, to explain to her why his head was under Penny's skirt. And, once again, he penetrated a wood where the sun could hardly pierce the thick canopy of the foliage. Though the shade was welcomed by his flesh, it blurred his eyesight. For fear of bumping into a tree, he waited for his eyes to adapt to the tangled gloom.

As he waited, he pulled the almond blossoms out of his hair and called his daughter's name: "Irene!"

An echo replied: "Victoria!"

He shouted his daughter's name again.

Again the echo replied: "Victoria!"

What was the meaning of this?

He could see more clearly now, and deep between the trees he made out a moving figure. A woman's figure, dressed up as a can-can dancer, waving her arms at him.

"What?" he called out. "You've seen my daughter?"

"She's on her way to the Royal Victoria Hospital."

He recognized the voice first. It was the voice of Marilyn Monroe.

"Why?" he said, walking towards her. "Irene is not due for another two months. Was it the shock of seeing me under Penny's skirt?"

"There's nothing wrong with Irene," said the dead movie star, flashing her luminous girlish smile. "She's on her way to the Royal Vic because your wife is heading there with you, in an ambulance."

"Ach! I told Xavier to tell her to send the ambulance back. Damn tenants. They only think of their own comfort. Which way is it to the Royal Vic? I must tell Yolanda not to let them wake me. I have so much to do yet."

Marilyn Monroe pointed coyly to the bulge in his pants. "You can't show yourself to Yolanda with that, honey. What will she think after Irene tells her about what she saw in that glade?"

He had forgotten his erection. He thanked Marilyn for pointing it out to him, then tried to see in his mind's eye some unpleasant scene — the Devil's grandson dancing on his grave, for instance — that would soften his erection; but in vain.

The movie star took pity on him and his predicament. "I'll alleviate it," she said. "I can alleviate you of anything, even guilt, and fill your heart with new dreams."

She knelt before Lukas. Then, pursing her plump purpled lips, she whispered to the bulge in his pants: "You'd have to be a pretty terrible cock to be so mean to a sweet and generous guy like Lukas, who's always treated you with the utmost kindness and consideration, attending to all your needs and wishes. Please go to sleep. Yolanda might think that you can rise with that bygone zest anytime you want, except when you're in bed with her. How could you do that to a woman who's been so nice to you?"

The bulge was still there, hard as a bone.

"Gee, Lukas," the dead actress said, "a gal like me almost never gets to meet so much resistance. Most cocks find it very difficult not to come at the sound of my voice."

"Don't take it personally, Miss Monroe. I've been dogged by ill fortune ever since the Devil's grandson gave me the evil eye, and nothing works as I want it to."

"Take heart. I won't let you down. What would you think of me? I want you to recover your zest for life and remember me always as the one who helped you recover it. Let's see. I can't stroke it, or put it in my mouth. Pardon me for saying so, but we mustn't touch — I'm a star. But I'll dance for you. You go behind those trees and massage it as you watch me dance."

Lukas had been lured to too many traps. So he said: "Why behind those trees?"

"You're so clever, darling, I'm sure you'll understand if you put your mind to it. What if Irene passed by again?"

That made sense. And although he had no desire to massage his penis, he hid behind a tree. Marilyn Monroe placed her hands on her hips, adopted the pose of a can-can dancer, and started crooning and waving her head and eyebrows, shaking her hips and raising a leg, then turning round and lifting her dress, stooping low to show her rump, the long feathers in her hair, in her bosom and round her waist emphasizing every one of her lewd movements as they beat the air like the wings of a hen trying to excite a rooster.

Ach, Lukas groaned as he grabbed his fly. Why do such things happen now, when I have neither the time nor the heart for them?

"So you thief," a voice said just then into his ear, "you could not cheat Death out of your life?"

Lukas froze in place. Except for his erection, which melted away instantly.

23

ALL AROUND, FROM the trees bending over him, men and women were hanging by their feet like the ghostly shapes of enormous bats, their eyes brooding and level with his own, looking at him upside down. Who were these creatures? Were they forest ghouls? Did Marilyn Monroe know about them when she sent him into their dark, wooded grave?

He looked at the face closest to him. It was that of his first employer in Montreal, Spiros Vrakas, the biggest thief of them all. Not only had he exploited Lukas as he exploited every new immigrant who worked for him, at the end he had also robbed him of three weeks' wages. But Lukas made no mention of that. He was more interested in finding his way out of that horrible forest and to the Royal Vic. So he said: "Why do you call me a thief, brother?"

"You know why. You think I don't know why? She told me everything. So drop the brotherly shit and tell me: Why did you do it? It couldn't have been the weight of my curses. Curses bring as much pain and retribution as the rope of a suicide brings good luck. Otherwise they would have expedited my wife here long ago. Why did you kill yourself?"

"I didn't kill myself."

"Still the proud one. No need to keep up appearances in this forest, you thief. All of us here are suicides."

"I'm not even dead. Only passing through."

"You're lying, just to piss me off!" Spiros said, his voice still a mere whisper. "You're one of us! You can't fool me! No one passes through this part of the forest unless he died or is dying of his own hand!"

"Show me the way out and you'll see that I'm not dead."

"Even if you had a chance to pull through, I never would show you the way out. Would *you*, if you were in my place? Look at me. Would *you* show me the way out of here if I'd condemned you to hang by your feet for all eternity, with nothing to gaze at but your own reflection in the pool made of your tears? I can't even communicate with the others and share my pain — our voices are reduced to a whisper. So talk to me. It's your last chance to lighten up the load that will hang from your feet. And believe me, it will be very heavy. Come on. The more you can take off before they hang you up, the better. Talk to me. Lighten up my load too. You owe me that much."

"Och, man, what is this song you're singing me? You killed yourself because your wife was dying for a kiss?"

"You could have said no."

"I was twenty-two. I hadn't kissed a woman in months."

"I hadn't kissed in three years."

"Maybe you should have."

Spiros, beyond himself now, said: "Don't tell me what I should have done. That's all I do here — hour after hour. Maybe I should have killed the bastard, I tell myself. Maybe I should have killed him the minute she told me, instead of taking her back to Greece." He sighed.

Unlike his words, his sigh echoed throughout the forest like the shudder of wandering souls. "I loved Montreal. But I went back. I even put the house I bought in Greece in her name, to show her that I'd forgiven her. To make sure I wouldn't regret it, I put her at the cash of the store I opened there so I could watch her all day. And to clean the fish, I didn't hire a Greek. I hired a Sudanese migrant worker who didn't know enough Greek to talk himself into a shithouse, let alone into her pants."

Tears were now streaming down his forehead and dripping into the small pool that had formed under his head. "My wife, for god's sake, a Greek woman from my own village, and the mother of my children, chasing me out of my own house to live with an Arab, and a black one at that! And again, hour after hour: I should have killed the two of them. Surely I'd have fared better for a crime of passion, even in my children's memories. But I was in such pain I couldn't think clearly. And to escape the pain I locked myself in my car, I turned on the engine, as you did —"

Lukas did not want to antagonize the cuckolded husband, but he could not let that slide. "I didn't turn the engine on," he said. "Why would I do such a stupid thing?"

"You still think I'm stupid, eh. Well, Stupid Spiros is going to have the time of his death knowing that you're hanging like him, upside down. Just the thought of it will lighten my load by at least twenty percent. If they hang you in full view of me, it might be reduced by half. So, you thief, why would I help you, even if you had a chance to make it to the Royal Vic and back to life? You're the best thing that's happened to me since I arrived here."

Lukas lowered his head. Obviously, like most people, Spiros believed more easily what is evil than good. So, feigning compunction, he murmured confidentially into his ear: "Ach, it tears my heart to admit such things out loud, but I must level with you. You guessed right. I didn't want to tell you, for fear you'd tell the others and I'd become the laughing stock of this forest."

Spiros's flow of tears ceased. "Go on, brother," he said, "lighten your load. I won't tell."

"I opened up a restaurant," Lukas said, speaking in whispers. "My wife gave me all the moral support I needed. She even gave me money. Why would a wife be so keen on her husband opening a restaurant, I often wondered. What woman would want to be married to a man who never gets home before midnight? Last night I found out what woman would want that."

Spiros's eyes were glowing now as they glowed once when he heard of other people's misfortunes.

"Ach," he said, smacking his lips. "I haven't felt this good in years."

Lukas thought: If life doesn't change people, you think death will?

Fortunately, by now, he had also discovered the dead's weak spot. So he said: "My only solace is that my children are old enough not to remember me only as a suicide."

Spiros's eyes grew dark again. His own children were too young when he moved back to Greece to remember anything of their father besides the circumstances of his death.

"If I show you the way to the Royal Vic," he said, "will you find my children and tell them of my life back in Montreal?"

"I will, on my sons' life," said Lukas, who had only one daughter.

"Go straight ahead," said Spiros, "then through the red gate at the other end."

Then, as Lukas walked away, he trotted out all the things he wanted him to tell his children, laying claim to more virtues, good deeds, even miracles, than Jesus himself.

24

AS THE GURNEY carrying her unconscious husband was wheeled into a trauma room, the first question the ER doctor on duty asked Yolanda was whether she knew how long Lukas had been in the garage.

"About three hours."

"Does he have any chronic illness, heart disease, anemia, or respiratory problems?"

"No, he hasn't even had a cold in years."

"He smokes?"

"Yes."

"Is he a heavy smoker?"

She hesitated, as if her answer might seal her husband's fate. But the doctor could not afford to wait. He said: "For your information, so you'll know: the longer a person breathes carbon monoxide, the worse the effects. It can kill some people after three or four hours. Heavy smokers are at a higher risk."

Then he rushed into the room where Lukas was hovering between life and death, leaving her alone with her anguish in the ringing silence of a long, deserted corridor.

How long ago was that? It was impossible to sense the passage of time in here. The dominant impression was stillness. Overhead banks of fluorescent tubes were putting out a cold light, turning the corridor with the green walls and the ivory tile floor into a shadowless blank. And in that blank stillness, her ears felt huge on her head, hungry for scraps of sound, while her mind jumped from one thing in the past to another thing in the present to another in the future. And that future seemed bleaker by the minute as she waited next to the door behind which they were trying to revive her husband. Yolanda was wide awake now, she could think coherently, yet, over and over, she envisioned the same scene in her mind's eye, always changing the ending: she was in bed, she heard the garage door open, then close, waited a few minutes, then went down to see what her husband was doing. As if their marriage could follow a route as fixed and sure as that followed by the train that took them on their honeymoon across Canada, all the way to Vancouver. It was Lukas's idea. He wanted to see his adopted country in all its breadth before he grew new roots in one of its cities. Death was far away.

She jumped out of her seat. She needed to do something, lest her thoughts drive her mad. So she approached the door and pushed it slightly open, if only to make sure her husband was still breathing.

Lukas was still breathing, but not on his own. His wrists and ankles held down by straps, he was surrounded by men and women in white coats, and monitors and gadgets to measure every bodily function. A tube was inserted down his throat and hooked up to a ventilator pumping air into his lungs. Never had she seen him so helpless, she thought, as she watched his chest rise and fall with every wheeze and whoosh of the bellows. But at least he was still breathing.

She shut the door. Then she thought of her daughter. How would she break the news to her in the morning? What effect could such news have on the baby she was carrying? Should she wait until Lukas's condition improved? What if it did not improve? Sure it will improve, she scolded herself. He's a fighter. So long as there's a breath in him he'll stay ahead of Death.

Finally she heard a door swing open. She held her breath. But the door was the one down the corridor that led to the reception area. A uniformed policewoman walked in. She asked Yolanda if she was Lukas's wife, then introduced herself, said she had spoken to her tenant and the paramedics, and now had a few questions to ask her.

The first question was the same one the doctor had asked her: Did she know how long her husband might have remained in the garage with the motor running? Unlike the doctor, however, the police officer frowned at her answer. She made no comment, but it was clear what she was thinking:

Yolanda knew her husband was in the garage for three hours, yet she did not check to see what he was doing down there, in the middle of the night. Suddenly every question from the cop became a trap.

"I thought he'd come up," she stammered defensively. "I was tired. As I waited for him to come up, I fell asleep. I guess he was tired too. Only he fell asleep in his car."

The officer made a note on her pad, then said: "How was your husband lately?"

It was Yolanda's turn to frown.

"Was he stressed, depressed or upset about something?" the officer expanded.

"No."

"Have you noticed any changes in his eating or sleeping habits, for instance. Did he talk, even jokingly, about suicide?"

"No! Why would you think that?"

"We found a bottle of sleeping pills on the front seat of his car."

"What?"

The only pill she had ever seen her husband take was the occasional aspirin, for a headache. And whenever he saw her take a sleeping pill because she was so stressed out by her work she could not sleep, he berated her.

"There was a bottle of sleeping pills on the front seat of his car," the officer repeated, her eyes zeroed in on Yolanda's, as as if there were deep secrets lurking in them. "There's one pill missing," she added.

Yolanda felt woozy, and leaned against the wall, her eyes fastened still on the officer. But for a moment, what they saw was Voula tut and shake her head as she related that night's events to every one she met. She too had probably noticed the sleeping pills, and by noon the whole neighbourhood would know about them. Not only because her tongue was the strongest and busiest muscle in her body, she also had a crush on Lukas, and she would be too happy to tell everyone what a bad wife he had. Why else would he try to kill himself? she would ask, knowing how much the whiff of scandal excites people in general, and Greeks in particular. For a week, at least, she would be the star of the community.

"Think please," the officer said.

Yolanda could only think of Voula. She should be grateful to her tenant, she told herself. If it had not been for Voula's nose, Lukas would be dead now.

"Four times more people commit suicide by intentionally poisoning themselves than die from unintentional CO poisoning," the officer continued. "The majority are men. Some leave a note. Your husband didn't. Was he upset about something lately? Did he manifest any feelings of sadness or depression? Any drastic personality changes?"

She shook her head no. "I see no reason, no reason at all. On the contrary, he was looking forward to the birth of our first grandchild. Every time he mentioned it, his face lit up."

But after the officer left, telling her that the CO alarm in her garage was defective and should be replaced, her mind went racing again, this time back to the last few weeks. Lukas seemed older and more weary than she had ever seen him. He reminisced about his childhood more often than he usually did. He even whispered in his sleep the name of a girl he had known back in Leros, in primary school. She had not pried any further, not only because she trusted him, but also because she knew from experience that if Lukas had something to say, he would say it of his own accord or there was no power on earth that could make him say what he had decided to keep secret.

Was he keeping something from her? Had she been wrong to impute his sudden burst of nostalgia to the excitement stirred by the upcoming birth of their first grandchild? What if the name he had whispered in his sleep was not the name of a girl he had known in his childhood? What if it was the name of a woman he was having an affair with now? Maybe that woman had broken up with him because he would not leave his wife. No, that did not make sense.

Some men, like Claude Martin, who had invited her and Lukas to the premiere of his play, viewed suicide as a thrilling, once-in-a-lifetime experience. Not Lukas. He was made of the same stuff as her own parents. Life had made them, like their parents and the parents of their parents, as stoic as a cactus. These people died of many things, and suicide was not one of them. Let alone over love. They would kill for love. But not themselves. Never themselves. Unless they found they had a terminal disease. That would be more in character. And he smoked too much. She kept nagging him to quit. Now had he found out he had lung cancer? Or Alzheimer's? She remembered clearly, upon leaving their daughter's baby shower, that he could not remember where he had parked his car.

She took a deep breath. Whatever Lukas had found out he had, only his doctor could confirm it. But she could not call his doctor now, in the middle of the night.

She groaned at the thought of having to wait another four or five hours to know the truth when she remembered that Lukas had come home from his poker game earlier than usual. Now these were people she could call at this hour. Lukas had given her their number, in case of an emergency.

Even if her husband was not the sort to kill himself over money, by the time she reached the public phones in the reception area, she had prepped herself for any outcome.

She had guessed right: the men were still up, playing cards. But the guy with the Chinese accent who answered the phone told her that Lukas had opted out that evening, that he had not seen him since their last game, a month ago.

Yolanda did not even think after the man hung up. She immediately dialled the number of Lukas's maître d', Marcel Peras, waking him up as he was going to sleep, to ask him if he knew why her husband had opted out of the poker game.

She had known Marcel for more than twenty years. He was almost part of the family. So off the top she told him what had happened, then asked him if her husband had shared with him something he might have kept secret from his wife, something that was serious enough to drive him to suicide.

Like Yolanda, Marcel had noticed lately that Lukas had been acting a bit weird, but nothing worth worrying about. There was nothing else, he concluded. If there was, he knew nothing about it.

"Call his poker partners," he suggested.

"I did. He didn't show up tonight."

"That's strange. He left at the same time he always leaves for his poker game. And when I wished him good luck, he thanked me, saying that he'd need all the luck he could get tonight."

When Yolanda hung up, she felt so confused that the tears she had held back till then finally welled in her eyes. It was still dark out there, outside the large window of the reception area. As dark as it had been the night Lukas had driven her to the hospital after her water broke. It was long ago, when she was young and unfamiliar with pain. And she went through so much pain that night that she said: Never again.

"Who were you talking to?" she heard her daughter say.

She thought she was hallucinating. But when she turned round, Irene was staring at her, one eyebrow raised, like her father. Alex was standing a few feet away, talking to the receptionist.

"Who were you talking to on the phone?" Irene repeated. "Your lover?"

25

THE VEGETATION FINALLY opened up, revealing a red gate. But Lukas was not the more relieved for it. He did not show it, in order to extract the information he needed from Spiros, but he was quite upset by the man's sad end and his own part in it, even though his former boss had been one of the meanest men he had known.

"Ach," he sighed. "I came to right a wrong and, so far, I've only caused pain and anguish to my daughter, my wife and my best friend, and added to my guilt. And I haven't found a shovel yet, let alone Zephira."

Then he stopped. A tricycle was standing a few feet from the gate, next to a bush. A tricycle very much like the one he used to ride faster than the wind, back in the wide and flat streets of Lakki, at an age when his heart was free of grief and remorse. He looked at it with nostalgia, when suddenly he saw some twigs shake and sway behind the bush. Which was strange, considering that there was not a breath of wind and everywhere else the twigs and the treetops stood rigid. Was someone hiding behind this bush? Was it the child riding the tricycle? Why had he left it there? Was he forced to?

Lukas stretched his neck over the bush and saw a small clearing. Its floor was covered with a tangle the colour of human flesh. On first sight, it looked like a swarming of oversized maggots feeding on an open wound. He thought of the child. If, for some reason, he had gone behind that bush, those huge maggots would eat him alive. He had to save him. But the more he looked at that moving mass, scanning it with his eyes for the child, the clearer he could see its outlines and movement. These were not maggots, but a sea of thrashing limbs, faces, breasts and bellies, backs and asses, quivering with life and moving, it seemed, to the beat of the same inner song.

He took another step forward. Now he could make out whole bodies entirely absorbed in one another. Two figures whose thrusting and clutching and biting and licking were akin to the cannibalistic, but drew only saliva, sweat — every bodily fluid except blood. A woman was picking her way between the bodies of men lying on their back, squatting over one, impaling herself on him as if she were riding horseback, then plodding across to the next. Another woman was lying on her back and pulling on her hair, while her partner pushed her head between her legs until it disappeared inside her. Next to them, a couple was fiercely engaged in the missionary position, the man's shaved head and broad back rising and falling over a woman whose head was thrown back and flinging from side to side, her mouth wide open.

Lukas frowned. "Mother?"

At the sound of his voice, the man's back froze, his bald head turned around. It was the head of Benito Mussolini.

"Lukas," the woman said as she sat up, her eyes ablaze.

She rose quickly to her feet, pulling down on her skirt.

"I'm all right, my angel. I fell down and this gentleman was helping me up."

Then, smiling, but only with her lips: "Why aren't you riding your tricycle? Where is your grandmother?"

Lukas turned away.

"Wait, my pride," his mother cried behind him. "Let me explain."

Then, louder: "Someone wake him, please, before he tells his father!"

26

HE WAS RUNNING once again as he had been running, it seemed to him, ever since he had entered this land where one no longer controls events, but is controlled by them. But no matter how fast he ran, his pursuer kept gaining on him. So he jumped into a tree and climbed for his life, as he had not climbed since he had left his native island — much faster even than in those days — scraping his skin against the rough bark as he hauled himself up, pushing his way to the top. When he reached it, he sat on a branch — one higher than any branch that he had ever been on before — to catch his breath, while his heart pounded furiously.

Mussolini was crouched on the forest floor below, sucking on his own navel. As he sucked, his chest expanded and his body grew in size. To Lukas, this seemed as ominous as all the pounding in his own chest, especially at his age. So, as if it were within his powers, he wondered if he should jump to wake himself. Surely Zephira would understand and give him another chance to redeem what he considered to be the big mistake of his life. But his mother would be only too pleased to see him wake again, and pleasing his mother was the last thing he wanted to do. Just the mere thought of her cheating on his father — and with the father of fascism! — while she would not let her son talk to his childhood sweetheart, stirred such pain in him that he cried out: "Bitch! I'll wring your heart just as you've wrung mine!"

The dead dictator let go of his navel, looked up at him, and said: "Sh-hh!"

But Lukas would not be silenced. "Those Sundays with my grandmother in Lakki," he went on to say, as if his mother could hear him, "were the happiest moments of my childhood. But you had to tarnish their memory as well!"

"Sh-hh!" Mussolini said again, this time with such force that his breath shook the crowns of the trees.

Lukas squeezed the branch he was perched on between his legs, holding tight to it with both hands.

But Mussolini's breath quickly died down, his chest deflated and his body shrank back to its normal size. He went back to sucking his navel again, as if it to draw from it the air he needed to shake Lukas off his branch and make him crash back to consciousness.

While Mussolini sucked and grew again in size, Lukas looked around for an escape route, and his eye caught sight of something moving at the other end of his branch. At first he thought it was a leaf. Then he realized it was a hand sticking out of a hole on the side of a cliff that was mostly hidden by the trees. Behind the hand — he could not believe his luck! — he saw Aris's face. His friend was pointing to the branch Lukas was sitting on as if to tell him that it was long enough to lead him to him. But it was barely large enough for one foot, and Lukas's head reeled at the thought of walking on such a narrow branch, perched up so high in the sky. However, he could drag himself along it to his peerless friend and to safety. So, slowly, he dragged himself forward. But Mussolini guessed his intentions, and he blew the air accumulated in his lungs with such force this time that the branch Lukas was crawling on swung so violently that he could no longer move. In panic he cried out to his friend to fly out and rescue him.

Aris just waved back.

He's probably chained, Lukas thought.

Mussolini was sucking on his navel again, one eye cocked now at his prey.

Lukas had to stop him from drawing any more air. But how? Suddenly he remembered how sensitive to flattery the Italian dictator was. He only hoped that, like Spiros, he was still unchastened by his experience and had not learnt that flattery is dangerous when you drink it straight.

"Duce, is that you?" he said, dissembling surprise while his mind raced to find some compliments to throw at that horror of a man who still carried the taste of his mother's body in his mouth. "O thanks to be to God a thousand times — it is you!"

Mussolini cocked his ear.

"Forgive me if I didn't recognize you," Lukas went on to say, inching his way towards Aris. "My mind was clouded by the memory of the girl I'm looking for. And you know better than anyone what such thoughts can do to a man when they obsess his mind as well as his heart to the exclusion of all else."

Mussolini let go of his navel.

"Yes," Lukas said, dragging himself forward, "you had to have the strength of a bull to satisfy them all. Even your father would have felt inadequate. And God knows what a womanizer he was!"

Mussolini threw out his chest and opened his mouth, but only a soft breeze blew out of it this time.

"Aris," Lukas called out, only six feet now from his friend. "Look who's here."

Only five feet to go.

"It's that genius of a man who was once Alexander and Caesar and Napoleon all in one, and whom the leaders of the West called the Saviour and those of the East called the Superman."

Only three feet to go. Down below, his arms akimbo and his chin raised, Mussolini was waiting for more. But Lukas was out of compliments. So he said to his friend: "Help me!"

Aris just looked at him and smiled.

"What's the matter with you?" Lukas said. "Give me something I can throw at this windbag!"

He was so wired up that his voice had risen in pitch. And Mussolini, upon hearing his last words, flew into such a rage that his wail raised a storm that shook the entire forest and made the branch Lukas was sitting on swing so violently that it began to crack. Still, Aris stood there, smiling. And Lukas was about to plunge headlong into the abyss that stretched underneath like a boundless deep when the storm stopped as suddenly as it had started, and all was still again.

Lukas looked down.

Mussolini was now eyeing a figure standing naked a few feet away. The naked figure of a young girl with a crown of dark and curly hair spread loosely around her head.

Zephira had come to his rescue once again. But once again she did not so much as turn her head towards the man risking his life to deliver the message he was bleeding inside to give her. Instead she turned and ran, with the father of fascism on her heels.

27

LUKAS CRAWLED THROUGH the opening and found himself inside a cave. But the joy of his close escape was dampened by the last image of Mussolini chasing the Amazon, the state in which he found his dearest friend again, and his own failure to bring him the shovel he needed to save his life.

Aris was not chained. However, his body was covered with mud and dust and his fingers were blistered and bleeding, as if he had been trying to dig his way out of his cell with his hands. Yet he was smiling.

"I've found her," he finally said, his eyes shining with delight.

"Who?"

"Artemis."

Lukas hugged him and kissed him on both cheeks, so happy he was that his friend had finally achieved his most cherished childhood dream. He was also happy for himself — he had one less thing to feel guilty about. Moreover, now that Aris had found the temple, Lukas was sure he would help him rescue Zephira from Mussolini. Lukas might even find time to do all the other things he wanted to do before he went back to carry on with his life.

But his friend wanted to first show him the temple he had found. He led Lukas through a dark passage and into another cavern. This one was larger and lit by a single candle burning on the beaten floor, which cast deep shadows against the walls. Lukas surveyed the scene and saw only a white toilet bowl, standing out sharply against the greyness of the rear wall, with no seat, no tank, no plumbing.

"There," Aris whispered with a rapt smile, pointing to a mound of clay.

Lukas did not notice it at first sight because it was the same colour as the beaten floor. He took a closer look. The mound of clay had the shape of a reclining female figure, her arms crossed and pressed on her bosom and her legs straight and close, like an effigy on an ancient tomb. As he stared at it perplexed, Aris knelt beside it and gently blew a speck of dust from its breast. Then, as if it were a beloved woman asleep in his bed, he slowly let his hand brush over her curves, then he pressed his face against her shoulder, and there he let it rest, breathing in with delight the smell of her clay hair, murmuring tender sounds into her ear.

For a moment, Lukas too surrendered to the spell cast by the light of the candle. For as it flickered, it created such shadows on the figure's face that it seemed to be alive and to respond to his friend's whispered sounds, so beautiful and proud was it carved.

Poor Aris, he thought, his heart heavy again. He has lost his wits waiting for the shovel, and out of clay, he has sculpted the goddess he could never find.

Just then a group of men carrying torches entered the cavern. They had the severe, hard faces of soldiers on duty, though they wore no uniform. Some of the faces were familiar. One was Vlassis, a boy from Leros with whom Lukas had done his military service on the Albanian border. Smart, with the clipped arrogance of a young corporal who for the first time in his life was furnished with full powers over other men, he said to Lukas: "Have you brought a shovel, you cock-sucking jerk?"

Taken aback by the vehemence of his tone and choice of words, Lukas searched for a diplomatic answer.

"No need for a shovel," Aris said. "I found her."

His words were greeted with catcalls and mockery.

"Is she a good lay?" Vlassis said, tickling the reclining figure's pubic area with the tip of his boot.

Aris flung himself at Vlassis's feet and kissed his boot, pushing it away from his goddess with his lips.

Vlassis withdrew his foot. But only to pick up momentum on the backswing and thrust it with a violent kick between the clay figure's thighs.

Aris shrieked with horror at the sight of the clay pelvis and lower abdomen crumbling back into dust, then fell on his violated Artemis. His cries came without words, bouncing from one damp wall to the other, as if they were looking for a hole to escape into open air, while the men looked on, snickering and jesting.

"Flush the butcher's little shit!" Vlassis bellowed.

Trampling the little mounds left of the clay goddess, two men dragged Aris towards the toilet bowl.

Lukas wanted to intervene, but he was brutally hurled aside. When he swayed back on his legs, the men filled the cavern and he could no longer push his way through to his friend. So, his back against a wall, he watched helplessly as Aris was shoved, feet first, into the toilet bowl, his arms held steady and tight against his body. Two, three, five pairs of hands pressed down on his head and shoulders to squeeze him into the hole like a piece of meat into a grinder, while the others repeated, like a mantra, "Shit back to shit! Shit back to shit!" the hollow vaults of the cavern deflecting their words back like amplifiers.

"He's a man!" Lukas cried out, adding that Aris had grown up with them, attended the same school, dived off the same rocks, but all eyes remained fixed on his friend, their endless chant transforming the cavern into a sound box, and the sound box into a collective brain.

Lukas knew he would be next. He searched with his eyes for the exit. It was blocked by more men pouring into the cavern to watch the spectacle, chanting like the others, "Shit back to shit!" All he could do now was wait for his turn to be flushed down the toilet.

Suddenly, as if he were waking back to life, Aris freed one hand, grabbed the rim of the bowl and hung on to it with all his might. Another pair of hands tried to pull it away, but they could not undo his grip. So a boot was lifted, and it came down on the fingers with such force that a crack appeared on the rim itself. Aris's cry pierced the chanting, but it was his last, for his executioners, taking advantage of his pain, pushed him further down until his torso disappeared into the bowl up to the neck. Presently Vlassis pulled on a chain hanging from the ceiling, and a flash of water splashed Aris's face, filling his mouth. Some of it gushed out and spurted the clothes of the men closest to the bowl. Furious at being splattered with shit water, one of them swung his torch through the air and clouted Aris in the face. The others hammered his head with the soles of their boots until it disappeared into the hole with a gargling sound.

"Shit back to shit," they said, their fury spent.

Then there was total silence, inside the bowl as well as inside the cavern, while all eyes remained fixed on the toilet, as if everyone was expecting it to back up. It did not back up, and the men at the entrance, their frenzy diminished, dispersed one by one.

Should he make for the exit now? Lukas wondered.

Too late. Two men had already grabbed his arms.

28

LUKAS DID NOT plead for mercy. He would not give them that satisfaction, and whatever horror they had in store for him, he felt he deserved it. But of all the horrors they could have put him through, never would he have expected to be led to his mother's grave and ordered to ask her forgiveness.

His mother was lying in her coffin, her face haggard, her hair dishevelled. Nestor's parents were at her side. His father, the priest, was swinging his censer to the accompaniment of incantations and hallelujahs, while his wife rubbed rosewater on the coffin-ridden woman's face and neck to refresh them.

"Look what you've done to your mother," she said, shaking her head at Lukas with disgust.

"Repent, my son," the priest said. "For sending your mother to her grave, for not giving her name to your daughter, for never holding a service in her memory."

"Not even a good thought," his wife added, "on the name day of she who bore him nine months and, if only for that, deserves a prayer and an offering every single day of his life."

The men forced Lukas to kneel beside the coffin.

"You won't leave this grave," Vlassis said, "or see your child again until you've asked your mother's forgiveness."

Of course Lukas wanted to see his child again, but he could not make himself say the words they wanted to hear. When he looked at his mother, only one word came to his mind. But he could not say it in the presence of strangers, though he itched to spit it in her face. Instead, he said: "I want to see my daughter again, but on her life, I cannot and will not make myself repent before the guilty."

"He's up to his tricks again," the priest's wife said, "trying to fool us with double talk, for there is only one guilty party in here, and it is him."

"Flushing a man down a toilet is not a crime?"

"He got his comeuppance. If that heathen hadn't chased Apostle John, my husband would have become head of the greatest monastery in Greece and died head of the Greek Orthodox Church, maybe Emperor of all Christendom!"

The priest told his wife to calm down. They had come for the benefit of an afflicted mother, he said, not to cause more mischief. Then he signalled the men to leave the grave.

"You and your wife should leave as well," Lukas said. "You could have prevented Aris's death, and you didn't."

"He deserved to die!" the priest's wife cried out again.

"Come along, woman," her husband said. "Let us give mother and son some privacy."

"How will we know that he has repented?"

"The grave's door will not open again unless Lukas's mother is satisfied."

Thus Lukas found himself alone with his mother. Whatever the feelings he harboured towards her may have been, his heart sank to see her so sick, distressed and disoriented. Knowing her, however, it could have been a ploy to soften him up and obtain from him all she wanted without conceding anything. He could not help admire her cunning and her tenacity. Even in death, she would not give up her resolve to keep him away from Zephira.

But now he had a card up his sleeve. If he played it right, he might even get his mother to take him herself to the Amazon's grave. So he steeled himself against pity, and said: "I swore on my daughter's life that I will not repent before the guilty. And you're guilty, if only of Aris's death. Had you not stopped me on the waterfront from speaking to Zephira, Aris would be alive. Then again, if you don't care for the life of your own son ..." He shook his head. "How could you do it, knowing all the while my life was in danger?"

His mother fixed her feverish and swollen eyes on him. "Why didn't you call me to your rescue? You turn to your grandmother for advice. You give her name to your daughter. Couldn't you turn to me once? Was my crime so horrible that your only thoughts of me should be groans and reproaches?"

"If only you knew how often I've wished for a mother I could shower with thanks and blessings. Was she truly as I remember her, I'd wonder, questioning my own memory. No more. For I'll always have the image of that clearing to remind me that you're capable of breaking even that most tender, most generous and most faithful heart of any man I've known."

His mother propped herself up. "Don't you lecture me about fidelity! As to your father's heart, if it's broken, I'm not the one who broke it."

Lukas decided to use the card he was keeping up his sleeve. "I haven't told him. Not yet."

"You yelled it from atop a tree, for all to hear. Benito begged you to keep quiet, but all you could think of was getting back at me by setting your father against the one person who loved him, consoled him, and nursed him to the end. Even in death I'm the only one who thinks of him still, though he won't visit me even when the almond trees are in bloom. Too busy looking for his parents." Tears sprung from her eyes. "What am I going to do now with my desires, and with no man to think of me — not even my prince?"

His impulse was to take her in his arms and stem her tears by telling her that he will think of her, and always with tenderness now. But what if she had made it all up, to keep him away from his father and obtain from him that which so far he would not concede to her? To test her, he said: "How can I make it up to you?"

"Too late for that."

"Then why did you tell them to bring me here?"

"I wanted to hear your voice one last time," she said, touching his face. "May your fortune be better than mine, my son. In life as in death."

Suddenly the door to the grave opened. She had forgiven him. He was free to go. Yet he did not move.

"What do you mean, one last time?" he said.

"Before your father's curse takes effect."

"What curse?"

"That every time I think of a man other than him —"

Suddenly a mothball popped out of her mouth.

"It's starting already," she moaned. "Why did you have to come looking for her? Such things ought to be left alone. Such things ought to be left alone," she cried again, as more mothballs popped out of her mouth, choking her.

Lukas tried to prop her up and tell her what his heart now ached to tell her, but the mothballs kept popping out so fast that within seconds, she was buried underneath them, and if he had not rushed out of the grave, they would have buried him as well.

29

THE AIR OUTSIDE the grave was cooler now and there was a scattered flock of clouds on the horizon, but Lukas only saw the last look of terror in his mother's eyes. And he knew it would haunt him until he found his father and made him take back the spell he had cast upon his wife.

His father's grave could not be far from hers. So he looked to the left, he looked to the right, and finally spotted his father on the roof of a chapel standing across the graveyard alley.

A ladder was leaning against the wall of the chapel. Lukas climbed its rungs with a heavy heart. He was supposed to return to his father with news of his parents, and take him out for a cup of coffee and a chat — he had brought him only pain. And he had no idea how to relieve him of it without twisting the knife in his wound.

His father was sitting at the other end of the roof, his feet dangling over the ledge. He was holding a fishing rod.

What could he be fishing for up here, on dry land?

His father turned and hushed him, pointing at the ground below. He did not seem pained at all. Did his mother lie to him, to win his sympathy?

When he leaned over the ledge to see what his father was pointing at, the first thing he noticed were the dead cats scattered at the foot of the wall, their skulls crushed. But that was not what his father was pointing at. He was pointing at a live cat approaching the carcasses and sniffing them cautiously, until it caught a whiff of the piece of fish hooked at the end of the line he was dangling over its head. When it finally approached the bait to smell it, Lukas realized what his father was doing and looked at him with as much astonishment as horror. As far as he could remember, he had never seen his father do something with sinister or malicious intent. What had brought about the change? Did his mother tell him the truth after all?

Suddenly a strident wail filled the air, and his father reeled in the cat, screeching and howling and clawing helplessly at the air as the hook tore into its mouth. Holding his rod now with one hand, his father picked up a brick with the other from a pile gathered next to him and smashed the beast's head, then unhooked it and threw it down among the other carcasses.

"You want to try?" he said to his son, as he hooked another piece of fish at the end of his line.

Lukas shook his head.

"It's all right. They have no heart — only a belly."

Lukas shook his head again.

His father cast his line.

Poor man. He whom nothing in life could defeat had gone crazy with pain over his wife's infidelity and was taking it out on the cats. One thing was sure, he did not know that his son knew, otherwise he would not look him in the face and smile. His mother must have only told him half the truth.

"Are you my father?" his father said, as he waited for the next cat.

"What?" said Lukas, thinking he had not heard right.

His father was about to repeat his question when he felt a tug at his line. The two men looked down. Instead of a cat hanging from the hook, they saw the black-clad figure of Nestor's father, accompanied this time by his hunchbacked sacristan. Holding the line tightly in his hand, the dead priest said to Lukas's father: "What are you doing? You want to get us all eaten by the rats?"

With his free hand, Lukas's father picked up a brick and hurled it down at Nestor's father. The priest dodged the brick, then ordered his sacristan to cut the line.

The sacristan cut the line with his pocket knife.

"If you start again," the priest said to Lukas's father, "I'll lock you up in your grave and throw away the key."

And he walked away, followed by his hunchbacked sacristan.

Lukas's father dropped the rod. "I want my mommy," he said, shaken by sobs.

Lukas had never seen his father cry. As he looked at the man of his childhood, so tall and sturdy, weeping like an abandoned child, a wave of shame went over him as though his father had died all over again, and he had killed him.

Holding back his tears, Lukas picked him up with as much ease as if his father were truly a child. Then, hugging him tightly in his arms, he carried him down the ladder, and into his grave where he laid him in his coffin.

"Close your eyes," he said, stroking his father's bald head, "go to sleep, and you'll find your mommy."

"All right!" said his father, flashing the one thing that had not changed and never changes — his smile. Then he curled up and shut his eyes like a child awaiting Santa's visit on Christmas Eve.

He had even robbed his father of his last chance to find the parents he never knew, Lukas told himself as he left the grave, his heart heavy with more guilt. Even if they managed to find their son, would he still remember his need of them?

30

HE MARCHED GRIMLY on, his head bent by the weight of his gloomy thoughts, until the earth beneath his feet ended abruptly and he found himself standing on an overhanging precipice. Had he reached the end of the cemetery?

The entire sky was now strewn with clouds. Stretching from under the lee of the rock he was standing on and as far as his eyes could see, there was a flat, treeless, steppe-like plain buffeted by the wind and covered, not by graves, but by gulls. Thousands of gulls, scavenging for food and wrangling over every edible piece they found. Could that be the sea he had emptied of its water? How different it looked from the one that had welcomed him upon his arrival, as the dawn of a new day was about to break.

What now?

There was no one else around. Only faraway on his left, a black pickup truck, little more than a dot, hurrying towards him on the sinewy road running along that desolate shoreline. When it reached him, he saw his son-in-law sitting behind the wheel, his face unusually sullen. Judy Yamada was sitting next to him, an expression of panic in her eyes.

"Get in the back," she said to Lukas.

His son-in-law gave him a dark look, then turned his face away. Did Irene tell him that she had seen her father under Penny's skirt?

"Why does Alex look so hostile and sad?" he asked.

"Irene's so upset about what you did, he's afraid she might have a miscarriage. Yolanda is beside herself too."

He groaned: Irene had told her mother as well.

"She thinks you've tried to kill yourself and can't understand why," Judy continued. "I tried to tell her that you didn't intend to kill yourself, she wouldn't believe me. Can you blame her? Who'd believe a thing like that? We all have such desires, you just don't act on them. A good thing I knew where to look for you."

Lukas smiled, relieved that his daughter had said nothing.

"I only took one sleeping pill," he said.

"They know that. They found the bottle on your car seat. What everyone is upset about is that after you took that pill you turned on the engine of your car."

Lukas lost his smile. Why would he do such a foolish thing, he said once again. This time, however, he tried to recall what exactly he did do in his garage. But his memories of his parents were still so vivid and painful that he could not see beyond them.

"Who are you looking for, anyway?" Judy said. "What dead are worth risking your life for?"

"I wasn't planning on dying," Lukas said, trying to make sense of all this.

"Well, you *are* dying. Even *they* know it," Judy added, pointing to the gulls hovering above their heads.

"They're sea gulls, not vultures."

"They're vultures. Sea gulls don't hover over the dying."

"If I'm dying because I inadvertently switched the engine on, switch it off and let me pursue my dream."

"They did switch it off. You wouldn't wake. So they rushed you to the hospital, to revive you. If we don't get you back into your body on time, you can kiss your dream and your life bye-bye."

"Jesus."

"Come on. Let go of the dead and climb in the back. I don't want to spend the rest of my life blaming myself for telling you about dreams."

Lukas tried to process all this in his head and come to a decision, but his mind was still too confused. So he asked Judy for a cigarette, to clear up the mess in his head.

"Get in the truck!" she shouted back. "This is not a question with multiple answers you have to puzzle over!"

Now Lukas was more determined than ever to find Zephira and alleviate at least some of the guilt accumulated in his heart. But how would he find her and get back to his body in time? Considering what had happened so far, he knew the odds were against it. Unless he called his grandmother to his rescue. So far he had not done that for fear that his mother would hear of it. Should he take that chance, he wondered as he moved to the back of the truck.

And he came face to face with the object of his obstinate pursuit.

"Send them away," Zephira said, dropping modestly her gaze from his probing eyes. "I'll get you back to your body."

Lukas banged on the truck. "Let's go."

The truck pulled away, its occupants thinking he was in it.

Lukas turned round to face the girl.

Zephira was no longer there.

He looked to the right, he looked to the left: the girl had vanished once again.

"What is the meaning of this?" he screamed. "What are you up to? This is no time for childish games!"

The truck was still in sight, speeding away in a burning cloud of dust, on the narrow, winding road that followed the coast, hugging the side of the precipice, high above the seabed he had condemned never to be licked by the tide again.

His first thought was: Why is Alex going so fast on such a narrow and sinewy road? Then he remembered that his son-in-law was rushing to the hospital to get him back into his body. And his truck was now pulling into a curve and about to disappear forever from his sight. Should he run after it?

Suddenly the small, stocky figure of a little boy appeared round the bend. To avoid the child, the truck swerved to the right and drove straight over the edge. A moment later, a crash louder than a crack of thunder shook the earth beneath Lukas's feet, this was followed by the appearance of a white cloud of gulls aroused by the crash and carried by their panic so high that they went through the blanket of clouds above, piercing it and unleashing torrents of rain.

Drenched, Lukas wanted to drag himself to the edge of the precipice, to look for a path among the rocks he could take to go down and pull the passengers out of the truck, in case by some miracle they were still alive. But his legs seemed as heavy as lead.

When he finally reached the edge, the torrents unleashed by the gulls had covered the entire seabed and the water was rising so fast he could no longer see the truck.

He stared benumbed at the raging surf dashing against the shore with a vengeance, rearing up and foaming like a demented army crying out again, "You're mine!"

The prospect of hanging all of eternity by his feet, next to Spiros, and suffering his sneers about Stupid Lukas causing so much pain and death for a girl, now seemed to him easier than facing his daughter and Judy's husband. All he had to do was fling himself over the edge.

Just then he heard a whisper. It came from the little boy who had sent the father of his grandchild and one of the smartest and sweetest women he knew to their death. He was still standing in the middle of the curve, buffeted by the rain and the wind, as if he were under the shock of the tragedy he had caused. Taking pity on him, Lukas went to him, and when he finally reached him, he shuddered: the boy was not human at all, but a doll. A well-contrived mechanical doll like those which say "pa-pa, ma-ma," only better constructed.

"What is this?" Lukas cried out with the terror of a man who is going out of his mind and realizes it. "What is going on?"

He touched the doll, to make sure it was not a hallucination. Instantly, as if his touch had triggered its mechanism, the doll waved its arms and its whisper grew louder. "You're mine," it said. "You're mine," it repeated, as Lukas stared at it aghast. "You're mine." Then it staggered away, repeating on and on the same dreadful sound, as the sky greyed and darkened and merged with the earth crouched now in death-like stillness, while the seething sea tossed itself in the air in a demented dance of reconquest and victory.

Should he follow the doll and perhaps find out who had put it there, on the curve? Or should he put that question too into the coffin of all the questions for which he must now accept that there would never be an answer, and jump over the edge and save himself more delusions and grief?

31

AS HE BATTLED with his dilemma, beaten by gusts of wind and rain, he saw in the sea of graves stretching on the other side of the road the small figure of his grandmother with her silvery-white hair tied as always behind her head in a neat bun. She had heard his call and come to his aid, as always, her white shroud flapping like a pennant of hope in the midst of the storm. She had even brought an umbrella.

"Come inside, child," she said, holding it over his head. "You'll catch your death."

He wanted to press her in his arms, kiss the beloved face that had occupied the most privileged place in his heart and in his memory, and share with her his grief. Instead, he said: "You should keep away from me. I only bring pain and sorrow to those who try to help me."

"You're the only one among the living who remembers me still," she replied. "Every time you call your daughter by her name, I live again. Do you think I'd let anyone rob me of that, I who've been through three wars, five epidemics and sixteen major earthquakes?" She took his hand. "My poor angel, your hand is as cold as mine."

He let her lead him through the graves and towards a faint light, as trustingly as he did when he was a child, knowing that if anyone could break his string of bitterness, it was her.

The faint light was coming from inside a burial vault. Lukas stooped, for he was tall and the vault's door low. After he passed through it, he saw two empty coffins set against the wall on his right, one on top of the other, like bunk beds. On his left there was a table and two chairs. His maternal grandfather, whose mane of undulating locks he had inherited, was sitting in one of them, elegantly gotten up in a dark suit, his moustache perfectly trimmed and of the same colour of mother-of-pearl as the mane that covered his head.

"Kiss your grandfather, my boy," his grandmother said, as she busied herself with a censer.

Lukas approached his grandfather, but the man turned his face away.

His wife shook her head. "Shame on you, Zacharia. Pouting — at your age."

"Look who's talking. He doesn't think of you one week, and you wish you were alive so you could kill yourself."

"The boy was only eight when you left us."

"There were pictures of me. The stories you told him — unless you lied."

"I did not lie. Tell him, Lukas."

"Every day she told me something about you," Lukas said.

"Some stories they must have been if they don't merit one thought."

"Oh stop pouting and light these coals," his wife said. "We have no time for such trifles. The boy's life is at stake."

Her husband threw his lighter on the table. "He's your joy. You save his life."

"Grandfather," Lukas said, "I think of you at least once a day."

His grandfather turned to him again, and, suppressing a smile, he said: "You do?"

Lukas's grandmother frowned. "Once a day?"

"It's maybe a small thought," Lukas told his grandfather, "that's why you don't catch it. But I think of you every time I comb my hair."

"Hmm," said his grandmother.

His grandfather lit the coals. As he blew on them, he said to his wife: "What are *you* pouting about? Get on with it. We've wasted enough time."

Lukas pulled one of the candles he had bought out of his pocket and offered it to his grandmother.

"A present," she said, her noble face with its network of tiny wrinkles smiling again. "Look, Zacharia, he brought me a present. And it's the same colour as my shroud."

She kissed Lukas on both cheeks, then told him to sit down on a chair. After he sat down, she pulled a hair off his head and placed it on the coals. While an acrid fragrance of grilled fish wafted over the room, she blew the resulting smoke from the censer into his face.

Half-choking, Lukas said: "Aren't you supposed to do this to the accompaniment of incantations?"

"Incantations?" his grandfather said. "She wants to get you back into your body, not turn you into a frog."

Lukas jumped off his chair. "I can't go back to my body."

"You must, my heart. Your time hasn't come yet. You have a lot to do still. Please sit down."

"No, I can't go back without Alex and Judy. You must help me find them. Had it not been for your stories, they'd have never come."

"I never said you could use dreams to change the past, my angel. Come for a visit — yes. But undo history? No one can do that. Talk to him, Zacharia. Put some sense into his head."

His grandfather said: "You can only mend things by leaving this place, now. Zephira — and with good reason, I might add, but that's another question — lured you here to torture you."

"Zephira? Aside from Aris, she's the only one who has lent me a hand."

"Think, please. Every time she helped you out of a bind, what happened afterwards?"

Lukas thought, and for one short moment he was brought face to face with something so unexpected, so final and so distressing that he rejected it outright, to save himself from that last indignity of seeing himself and his offer of atonement and reconciliation rejected by Zephira as slightingly as the sea rejects a dead fish. But rather than accept defeat and cut his losses as he would have normally done, he let the pain and anger and humiliation welling up in him since he had embarked on his dream blind his judgment, and when he spoke again, he lashed out at his grandmother.

"You knew of her intentions," he said, "yet you let it all happen. Why? So all my other memories would be poisoned and I'd think only of you? Even if it meant breaking my father's heart?" He pointed at his grandfather. "Him, I could understand. He never liked my father. You told me yourself. He never wanted his daughter to marry an orphan with no education, no money and no pedigree. But you, whom my father loved as a mother! I bet you even knew what your daughter was doing when she would send you and me off to Lakki to ride those cursed tricycles."

"Not true," his grandmother muttered, shaking her old head. "None of it is true."

"Then why didn't you warn me about Zephira?"

"Would you have believed her?" his grandfather said. "Would you have given up your trip? Now sit down. You've caused yourself and others enough pain."

"Please, sit down, my angel," his grandmother said. "Sit down and let go of the old rancours. Let go of them, my sweet. Otherwise you'll end up like Zephira, with only bitterness in your heart. So much bitterness that your mother's curse came true. Let go of the past. The more you hold on to it, the worse it will get, and the more you'll make up vexations and afflictions that didn't even occur. Sit down. Please. Sit down and let me get you back into your body before it's too late."

Lukas looked down at her. He wanted to ask her what curse had his mother cast upon Zephira, but all he could say was: "What — you're afraid I'll die and there will be no one left to remember you?"

"Stop it, child," his grandmother said. "Don't you see what she's doing to you?"

She was poisoning the only memory of his childhood left unscathed and the one he held most sacred, and cutting his heart into pieces with every word he threw at that tender-hearted woman who, for so many years, had loved him as only a grandmother can love. Yet he went on to say: "I only see this: If you'd come earlier, my son-in-law and Judy would still be alive. But you came to my rescue only when I was about to jump off that cliff."

He turned to go.

His grandmother grabbed his hand and kissed it, weeping and saying: "My joy. My only joy. Please sit down."

"You think I've got the heart to go back and face my daughter now?"

He pulled his hand away from her lips, and walked out without kissing her beloved face though he had always regretted not having been at her funeral to kiss it one last time before she was given back to the earth.

32

HE MOVED FORWARD, blinded by his feelings and guided by his feet, the rain and the wind lashing furiously at him again. The spring dawn that had welcomed him upon his arrival was now a distant memory, and the summer day that had followed seemed to have left permanently this land of bitter memories and heartbreaking encounters at the mercy of a cold autumnal dusk.

"How nice of you to remember me."

The voice was that of old Yakovos, the one-armed owner of the newspaper stall where he used to buy his Illustrated Classics. He was sitting, very thin and stooped, in the entrance of an ossuary, between a small table covered with dusty old magazines and a swivel rack carrying three post-cards and a folded map. A naked bulb was hanging from the ceiling, casting a pale and sickly light on his bald head.

"What will it be this time?" he said, as a swirl of dead leaves pulled along by the wind landed at his feet. "*The Odyssey*? *The Count of Monte Cristo*? *Moby Dick*? A map of the cemetery?"

Lukas shook his head. Even if a map could help him find Zephira, he would be powerless against her, and would remain so as long as he was alive. Once dead, he would need no map to find her and make her pay for all the woes of which she was the cause.

"How about some postcards?"

Lukas shook his head again. "What was the curse my mother put on the Amazon?"

"The second worst curse of them all. Tfou, tfou," the old man spat to his left and to his right, to ward off such curses from himself. Then he went on to say: "'May there be no one to close her eyes when she dies.' That is what your mother said, thinking you'd left Leros because of the Amazon. So when the Amazon passed away, no one was there to shut her eyes on the world to which she no longer belonged."

Lukas prayed that his wife and daughter would shut his eyes without cursing him, then asked the dead shop owner for a cigarette.

In the distance, dogs were heard howling, aroused by the smell of a dying body.

"We're going to have a new resident," the old man said, opening a pack of cigarettes.

"Yes — me."

"Why so soon? You're the only one left back there who remembers me still. Is it cancer?"

"No."

Old Yakovos gave him a cigarette and a match. "How about your monthly horoscope?"

"I'm dying!"

"The dead man's monthly horoscope. It tells you how you'll be remembered every day of the coming month."

"Is that all you dead care about?"

"What else is there?"

A whole life, he wanted to cry out. A wife, a child, soon a grandchild. Yet no one, not even the grandmother he once idolized, had inquired about them. Damn self-centred ghouls!

He paid old Yakovos and walked away.

The rain was pouring down again on his head, like all the tears he was fighting back as he recalled another lifetime. The wind was moaning and hissing among the graves, like cemetery gossips commenting on the new arrival. And now two dogs — large, shaggy and dark — stood, their legs stiff, across his path. They looked at Lukas, raised their heads, and howled.

"I know, I know. I just want to have one last smoke."

He wanted to smoke his last cigarette by the sea. But Zephira had also robbed him of that pleasure when she buried Alex and Judy in its depths, transforming the soft murmur of its rolling waves into a curse of her own.

"What the hell, it's raining, anyway."

He searched with his eyes for a shelter.

It had grown so dark he could hardly see further than the first row of gravestones. So, with the two dogs on his heels, he navigated through the graves, looking for a tree, an open tomb, anything that would keep his cigarette dry so that its smoke would relieve him of some of his bitterness and soften his passing. Eventually he reached the last structure in this part of the cemetery: a mausoleum standing on a solitary promontory projecting into the darkness of the sea. It was undoubtedly the largest burial accommodation he had seen so far, and its door was open. Yet he hesitated to go in.

Behind him the two dogs growled with a hint of impatience, as if to tell him to stop dilly-dallying and putting off the inevitable. He was dying — what further misfortune could befall him?

33

THE INTERIOR OF the mausoleum was swathed in pitch-black darkness. Three large windows ran across one wall. They looked out onto the dark-blue sea sprawling below like those of a ship's bridge. The waves lapping and splashing against the rock beneath them gave him the impression that he was back on the boat that had carried him away from his native island. That all that he had done in the ensuing forty years had been a mere daydream from that first crossing. He sighed, stuck the cigarette between his lips, and lit the match.

The light of the match revealed one bed. It was a large bed and its headboard faced the three windows. Propped up against the headboard was a woman. She was wearing a loose white tunic that covered half her body, in such a way that the parts covered seemed more alluring than the ones exposed. Her face was so handsome, her bearing so regal, that he thought he had stumbled upon the temple that Aris had been looking for. But this woman's skin was the colour of flesh, not marble. Was she another trap set by Zephira to persecute him even as his existence wore to its end, by jogging in him those joys and desires that make such farewells to life so agonizing? Should he leave? But to go where? He did not want to die in the rain, between two graves.

"Forgive me for breaking your solitude," he finally said. "I wanted to have one last smoke without getting my cigarette wet."

"Stay," she said. "I haven't combed a man's hair for a long time, and you have such a beautiful mane. After I comb it, you'll comb my hair. I can comb it myself, but that no longer gives me the thrill it once did."

There was such a kindliness in her voice, her face exuded such sweet serenity, that he wanted to put his head in her lap and end his suffering there. Yet he did not move when she invited him to sit on her bed. First he wanted to make sure it was not a trap. So he said: "I'd rather die in the rain like a dog than let my enemy unleash her wrath upon you for harbouring me, as she has unleashed it upon everyone who's been kind to me."

The woman pulled a comb from her hair, and said: "If your enemy is dead, you've nothing to fear. This comb can stop her from feeding on those memories from which the dead draw their power over the living. But if your enemy is still alive, you should leave, though I want you to stay. My comb is powerless against those things left unresolved but which can still be resolved."

He threw his cigarette out the window.

I'm such a sucker, he thought, as he sat on the bed, anticipating another blow, welcoming it even as further punishment for his gullibility, first for thinking that he could right the past and now for believing that a comb could release him from it and all the dead he had pained since he had embarked on his dream. One thing was sure, however: there was no one left he could still hurt, except himself. And the worst thing that could happen to him was about to happen any minute, when they would try to revive his body.

"I wasn't planning on dying," he said after he put his head on the woman's lap. "When I took that sleeping pill, dying wasn't even a remote possibility. Why would I want to die? I was content with my life — until Zephira's memory resurfaced again. I embarked on this dream to right what I'd done badly in the past and tell her what I'd left unsaid, so I could live in peace with my family the years left to me. Instead, I've tarnished my fondest memories. That must be the worst curse of them all — not to have one fond memory to fall back on as your future shrinks. The birth of a grandchild could give meaning to old age and soften its pains. But my daughter will never let me see my grandchild now. Is that a life worth going back to?"

What little illusions he had about the hereafter and its

rewards were blown away as well, and what he had seen so far of the dead only increased his desire to live. Yet, there was no more anxiety in his voice. There was only sadness now, deep and without hope, as he went on to say: "I was seventeen, for God's sake. It was a mistake, a cowardly mistake, but I was seventeen. How could a mistake made at seventeen cast a shadow on a whole life?"

The comb was now running softly through his locks, triggering little waves of sensation that started at the root of his hair and moved to the base of his skull, then along his nerves all the way to his toes, making his whole body tingle.

"How stupid everything seems when it fails," he said, grunting his pleasure now. "Might as well ask a refund for a lottery ticket because it didn't win."

Then he fell silent, as another rush of exhilaration unfurled across his skin. He closed his eyes to tend it better, nursing carefully what he felt. As the feeling grew, he felt so light and weightless and content that he thought that the woman was Death herself, because with every run of her comb, she was surrounding him with so much tenderness that he was convinced that soon he would see that famous tunnel with the bright light at the end that people who come back to life talk about.

Rather than bemoan his fate, he said: "At least, I will no longer be pursued by shadows I can't fight."

Then he felt himself move out of his body and slide over the side of the bed, but not down to the floor. He rose upwards, slowly. He stopped floating a moment, right below the ceiling, to thank the woman for helping him fly again, and saw himself stretched out on the bed below, his head tenderly pillowed on her lap. The woman was combing his hair and humming:

My love is as boundless as the sky,
and I've now someone to share it with.

Finally I've made someone happy, he thought. Then he drifted through a window and out into the night.

34

THE JOY OF flying was so strong that it liberated him from the prison of his memories and he revelled in his flight as in times past when he could soar higher than the highest buildings, dive and bank and make loops and rolls in the infinite host of worlds whirling round every night between the bed of his childhood and the stars of the Milky Way. He was so drunk with exhilaration that when he finally saw a bright light ahead of him in the night eternal, he thought it was the light at the end of the dark tunnel he had heard about so much. Rather than squirm away from the terrible finality of death, he moved forward, anxious to fly out into eternity.

But the light, he soon discovered, was shining through a window. The large front window of his restaurant. Like every night before closing, the chairs had been upturned in neat rows on the tables and the floor had been swept and washed. All that remained was to turn the lights out.

Hovering above the window, he peered inside to see who was closing tonight, and saw his wife. His first impulse was to fly away before the feelings of remorse which the flight had helped him shed crowded back in his mind and weighed down his body again. But Yolanda's face was so drawn, her eyes were swollen with so much anguish that he could feel her pain in his own heart. No, he told himself, he could not leave her in such despair, only to fly back to a complete stranger and make her happy. He should tell his wife how sorry he was for the grief he had caused her and his daughter. Tell her that it was all a stupid mistake, not a suicide. That he will do his utmost to make up for Alex's death. And that he will always love her. Yes, he must tell her all that.

He landed in front of the window.

Yolanda turned to the window and looked into the night, as if she had felt his presence.

Lukas took the second candle out of his pocket and said to her: "I brought you a gift. Light it if I annoy you in your dreams. I don't think I will. The dead shouldn't annoy those they love. Out of pity for them, they should stay dead. But you never know what death might do to me."

Yolanda's expression did not change. She kept her eyes fixed on her husband's face, as if she refused to acknowledge his present.

"My dearly beloved," she finally said.

Lukas's heart brimmed. She loved him still!

"I know you can hear me," she continued. "But will I hear your beautiful voice again? If not, what life is dear to me bereft of you? I've said these words before. You laughed, and are probably laughing at them again. This time you'll know they always came from the heart, because if I don't hear your beautiful voice again, I'll know I've lost you on this earth and I'll join you wherever you may be."

Lukas was not laughing at all.

"Don't be foolish!" he cried out. "You still have so much to live for. Besides, if you die, who will tell my grandchild about me the way I really was? Not my daughter."

Yolanda's eyes were still fixed upon him, yet her expression did not change. She could see him, he concluded, but she could not hear him through that window.

He turned to the door, felt for the latch, tried to open it, and the alarm went off.

"What's that?" Yolanda said from behind the window, trying to see through it into the night. "What's going on?"

Swearing, Lukas fumbled through his pockets for his keys. But he had left them in his car's ignition.

"We're losing him!" a tense voice cried behind him.

He turned and saw Zephira rushing towards him, followed by two men dressed in white rolling a weird machine mounted on wheels.

"Stop him!" she shouted to them. "If he goes through that door, we lose him for ever!"

Trying not to give way to panic, Lukas banged on the door, shouting to his wife to let him in. But Yolanda stood there, staring out the window at Zephira and the two men, and muttering: "Oh my God! Oh my God!"

When Zephira and the two men finally reached Lukas, the only way he could escape them was by rising upwards again.

"Come back!" Zephira shouted to him. "Do you hear — you coward — up there! Come back!"

The two men let go of the machine and grabbed Lukas's feet. Suspended in midair, he hurled the candle at them, he swung to the right and swung to the left, to free his feet; but all in vain.

"You're mine now!" Zephira said. "You're mine!"

Yolanda let out a heart-rending wail.

Still suspended in midair, Lukas turned to the window and saw his wife bury her face in her hands. Zephira is lying, he wanted to tell her; he was not hers. But his daughter appeared beside her mother, to clasp her tightly in her arms, as though to shelter her from her swinish husband and console her. And the dark look she gave her father was filled with such hatred and unutterable reproach that it sucked his soul out of him, and he collapsed, as if all life had left him.

35

LUKAS ADORED HIS daughter. Yolanda had never seen him happier or prouder than during his chats with Irene, when she taught him something he did not know. Irene loved her father too. So much so she hoped her baby was a boy: she had heard that boys take after their maternal grandfather. She even refused to look at the screen during her ultrasound scans, lest she discover that she was carrying a girl. But, Yolanda thought, that was not the reason why Voula was in such a hurry to call Irene and inform her of what had happened to her father.

"She dared wake you in the middle of the night with such news?" she cried out.

"I'm his daughter."

"You're pregnant! What was she hoping for — a miscarriage?"

"Is that why *you* didn't call me?"

Yolanda balled her fists in the pockets of her coat. The dread of losing her husband and the best friend she had, deserved, if not the support and consolation of her daughter, at least the respect of silence. But as soon as she arrived, Irene accused her of talking on the phone to some lover. If it was a joke, it was a bad one. But Yolanda let it slide. Her daughter was probably as confused and distressed as she herself was. At least that is what she thought until Irene, smug in her yet untested, hence unblemished, role as wife and mother, confronted her and said: "You were afraid I'll miscarry? Is that the only reason why you didn't call me? Better tell me now, before I find out myself."

Yolanda took a deep breath. She knew that if she did not clear things up now and, by some bad luck, Lukas did die, her daughter would never forgive her for falling asleep while he was locked up in his car with the motor running. So she said: "What is it, Irene? You reproach me for not doing what Voula did? I was asleep two floors above the garage, while she was next door to it."

Her daughter's face remained as tight and hard as that of a cop interrogating a suspect. Worse: she had become the mother-in-law Yolanda never had. And a mother-in-law with a law degree.

"If you were asleep, how did you end up in the garage?"

"I woke up. When I didn't see your father in bed, next to me —"

"What woke you up?"

"I woke up by myself."

Irene's scowl deepened.

"After she discovered dad in the garage, Voula banged on your door. That couldn't wake you up?"

"She never banged on our door. I'd have heard."

"Why would she lie?"

Yolanda's shoulders slumped as she realized that her daughter's faith in the woman who had rescued her beloved father was more important to her now than anything her own mother could say. Was that Voula's intention? Yolanda's mind drifted for a moment back to the garage: Voula had pulled her husband out of his car and called 911, without waking her, to obtain from Lukas the affection he would never lavish on her, by making his wife look bad, and by winning the gratitude and trust of his daughter, knowing how much Irene's opinion meant to her father. But how could she share her suspicions without being accused of wanting to clear herself by throwing mud at the woman who did exactly what had to be done to save Lukas's life?

"Did Voula also lie when she told me you were out last night with a man?" Irene went on, coldly, pitilessly. "According to her, a man dropped you off around eleven o'clock, and that you were slightly tipsy when you walked from his car to the front door."

Yolanda felt nauseous. "That pisspot!" she hissed. "That sycophant! Keeping tabs on me, sucking up to my husband and to my daughter by playing the good Samaritan, when she wouldn't even show up at the Second Coming if it happened on bingo night! I'm going to nail that muckraker's tongue to her palate, if it's the last thing I do!"

"Why? Because she tried to revive my dad, in the freezing cold, while you were in your warm bed, dreaming of your lover?" She looked at her mother with disgust. "At your age. Some grandmother you are."

Yolanda opened her mouth, more confused now by this sudden rearrangement of allegiances than by her daughter's vehemence. Holding back her tears, she said in a high-pitched voice, as if the roles had been reversed and she were the daughter: "I had dinner with Daniel Bouchard. He wanted to talk to me about a book he wants me to help him write. That's all."

"Why didn't you go to dad's restaurant?"

"This is ridiculous."

"Oh yeah? Let me tell you something, to show you how serious I am: If dad doesn't pull through, I swear, on the life growing inside me, you will never see my face again or the face of my child."

Then she walked away, while a siren wailed in the night towards the hospital where Yolanda felt trapped with a daughter whose heart was now filled with wrath and spite for her mother. How quickly loyalties change, she thought. One drop of venom and all my years with Lukas have turned into slime. I should make a note of that, for Daniel's book. Women are sometimes their own worst enemies. What am I saying? What book? If Lukas doesn't regain consciousness and put the lie to Voula's insinuations, that book will become the object of my shame. How could I work on such a book?

Suddenly another thought dawned on her, and her heart lurched in horror: What if, to shame her, Voula, in her twisted way, had called Lukas earlier in the evening to tell him that she had seen his wife drive away with another man? It would explain why he opted out of the poker game, yet left his restaurant early. No wonder Marcel knew nothing. How could Lukas, proud as he was, tell another man that he was on his way to spy on his unfaithful wife? Thus, even though she knew her husband was not the sort to kill himself over such things, Yolanda convinced herself that, parked in the darkness, he had waited until she came home, to check Voula's allegations. Hadn't he told Yolanda that Daniel Bouchard was in love with her? When he saw her get out of Daniel's car, depressed as he had been lately about his age, he concluded that his wife had turned to a younger man. He locked himself in their garage, eighteen feet under their marriage bed, popped a sleeping pill, and turned the motor on.

She was so ill with guilt by now that when she saw Marcel Peras walk through the main entrance, her first reaction was to hide. So she quickly moved towards the door leading to the corridor. As she did that, she knew that she would be hiding for the rest of her life: Lukas was known and loved by so many people that she could never go out again without bumping into one of them. Even if Lukas pulled through and never told anyone what had driven him to suicide, she was convinced that Voula would make sure they all knew, even her colleagues at school. But as she slipped through the door, the doctor called her. She had not seen him talking to Alex and Irene. When he stepped out from behind her son-in-law's greater bulk, holding a clipboard in one hand, she instinctively glanced at her daughter. Irene had buried her face in her hands. Next to her, Alex had lowered his eyes and was staring at the floor. Marcel too. When Yolanda turned her eyes back to the doctor, her heart was pounding inside her chest as if he were coming at her with a gun. Then everything started to swim around her, and all her thoughts and Irene's angry words were replaced by a buzz.

"Sit down, please," the doctor said.

She felt a hush descend on the room as if everyone and everything had stopped to hear her reaction to what the doctor was about to tell her. Even the intercom had fallen silent and turned into an ear.

She did not sit down. Instead she spoke. As if to forestall the inevitable, perhaps even change it, she spoke first and, her heart in her mouth, she said: "He can't die on me like this. He should know the truth first."

36

THERE WAS ONLY blackness before him now. And total silence. Was he dead? He ran a hand over his body, touching the different parts to see if they were still there. When he reached his head, he discovered that it was still pillowed in the woman's lap. He glanced up.

She gave him a tender smile, her face bowed over his.

"Am I dead?"

"Not yet."

He sat up.

She tossed her hair loose, and, her eyes shining with excitement, waited for him to comb her. But Lukas was so incensed by his latest encounter with Zephira that he could think of nothing else.

"That callous, heartless witch!" he said. "Now that she has poisoned all my memories and set my daughter against me, she has turned on my wife, saying in front of her that I'm hers and calling me a coward — I, who've risked my life to make amends to her! Ach, what a fool I've been! Not only have I lost the only person who loved me still, no one's left to defend my memory, and my grandchild, and his children, and the children of their children — they'll all and forever remember me only as the coward who brought grief to his family for the sake of a seventeen-year-old witch! Why did I take that pill! Why, on the way home, didn't I slam into a wall! At least I wouldn't have died unmourned by my wife. My friends and neighbours would have only good words for a man who died upon his return from work, exhausted. And my daughter would not be shedding bitter tears over her husband's casket and spitting on mine."

He turned to the woman. She was leaning back now, against the headboard, her eyes resting on the comb she was holding in her hands. Longing eyes, shining with tenderness and excitement a moment ago, filled now with an immense sadness.

"I thought you could protect me against the dead," he said to her, not realizing that his pain was caused not by what Zephira had said but that she had said it in front of his wife and daughter. "Why didn't you? I could have made that witch give back everything she took from me," he went on, the possibility that she could have helped him and did not driving him to even greater fury. "You were afraid that once I'd sorted out that little witch, I'd go back to my wife? What is it with you dead? Don't you think of anyone but yourselves? Or is it that you find our suffering amusing? Is that it? Is that how you amuse yourselves? By haunting and persecuting the living? And to think that I'm stuck with you now!"

He stopped, exhausted, but not relieved.

"Go," she finally said with a choked voice, her eyes still resting on her comb. "You have things to do yet."

He looked at her. If he could only get his hands on her comb. It would help him do all he wished to do and find the time to get back to his body and restore his reputation.

"Would you lend me your comb?"

She shook her head.

"I'll bring it back. Upon my word. I'll bring it back, and comb your hair. Please. It's a dying man's last wish."

She shook her head again. Obviously, here too a man could not get what he wanted without fighting for it even when he was dying. He tried another tack.

"You're right, what's done is done. I can change none of it. It's time I learned that."

He leaned back against the headboard, next to her. It was no longer raining outside, and through the drifting clouds he saw the full moon rising at the horizon.

"Forgive me for my evil thoughts and accusations. I could no longer weigh my words as I ought. I was hurt. And when the heart grieves nothing can make it listen to reason and we let our little sorrows blind us, even in the presence of great happiness. It won't happen again. I won't let that little witch rob me of you too. Yolanda — I could explain everything to her in a dream. I only hope Irene will overcome her grief quickly, find another husband, and remember the good things again."

Pause.

"You want me to comb you?"

She did not reply. Instead, she pulled some of Lukas's hair caught in the comb and threw the tuft into the air, towards the window on their right. Then, together, they watched the tuft go out the window, flutter in the breeze like a butterfly, then fly by the window in the middle, then by the window on their left, catching the moonlight on the way.

"How beautiful," said Lukas, thinking she was cleaning the comb before giving it to him.

Silently the woman pulled the remaining hair from the comb. And again they watched the tuft she threw in the air fly out the first window to the right of the bed, then, carried by the breeze blowing softly from the sea, past the second window, then the third window, catching the moonlight on the way.

He put his hand on the comb. "Let me comb your hair."

Her fingers were clutching the comb so tightly he could not pull it away.

"Please, let me comb your hair, and make peace."

He pulled again, this time with such force that he broke the comb in two.

The woman let out a gasp.

"I'm sorry," he said. "I'll mend it. Don't cry."

He wanted to seize her hand, both her hands, and kiss them, and now he gave a gasp: the woman's hands had turned as cold and hard as marble. He looked at her face: it had turned to marble too. And two tears were hanging on her eyelashes, as bright and tough as pearls.

"What have I done?"

He ran the piece of comb he was holding on her marble hair, praying that it would bring her back to life; but in vain. He tried to pull the other half from her marble fingers, so he could comb her with both pieces; but again in vain.

"Damn you, Zephira. You've also managed to ruin my last sanctuary and saddle my conscience with more regret. Ach! why didn't I comb her hair when she asked me to."

He sat there, shaking his head.

"How could I, at my age, let a seventeen-year-old girl make such a fool of me? She must be truly gloating now."

He got off the bed, seething with anger.

"Isn't there a limit to revenge? How could she find joy in torturing a man who can't fight back? At least there should be a limit to baseness! For you're base and vile, Zephira. Otherwise, rather than spend all your time hatching your dirty plots and hurting so many innocent people, you could have spared some of your witchery to obtain another grave for your poor father!"

He stared out the window. "All in good time. We'll see who the coward is when I'm dead and endowed with the same powers as you. Upon my word! — I won't relent in my vengeance until I've fitted your two feet into one shoe!"

He would have gone on venting the anger welling up in him till death had put a stop to it if his eye had not caught sight of a tuft of his hair hovering there, in the breeze, on his left, in front of the third window.

How strange. Was the other tuft still there as well?

He turned to look for it, and gave another gasp.

37

FURTHER TO THE left, coming from the darkness beyond, a flat-bottomed barge was approaching. Two figures were standing on it: one at the stern, manning the rudder; the other at the bow, pointing to the tuft of hair. The first was definitely a man. The second was definitely a girl. With a crown of hair spread loosely around her head. As the barge approached the windows, her upper body leaned forward, as if she were trying to look through the night inside the mausoleum. Lukas could almost feel her squinting eyes. He fell back a step.

Did the woman know his hair would hover outside the window like a lure? If she knew, why did she drop it? Because he would not comb her hair? Certainly she knew he was powerless against Zephira so long as he was alive.

The barge was floating in front of the windows, about seven metres from him. As he stood there in helpless silence, Zephira raised a storm lantern and swung it over the flat bed of her barge, as if to attract the attention of those invisible to her eyes in the shadows of that mausoleum.

Lukas took a step forward, to look at what she was trying to show him.

Two bodies, a man's and a woman's, were lying side by side at her feet, their chests open down the middle, each revealing a glowing purple heart that was still beating. He looked at their faces, and, in the stillness of that tomb, he thought that he was going out of his mind. The man was his son-in-law, and the woman, Judy Yamada.

Could it be another one of Zephira's tricks? She was probably afraid of the occupant of the mausoleum and her powers. Unaware that she had turned to stone, to lure him away from her, she had fished the two bodies out of the sea, and used some gadget to get the hearts beating, to make him think they were still alive and lure him to go out and rescue them.

But what if it was not a trick? What if they were alive? And he thought that no further misfortune could befall him! What more did she want of him? She had wrecked his life, she had wrecked his memories — would she not relent in her persecution of him until she had robbed him of his pride and of his senses as well? What good would he be to her deprived of his sanity? You can't persecute a man who no longer has any hopes, memories or fears. And these are precisely the food from which, like all the dead, she drew her power over him. The woman said so, and she was right.

Suddenly he smiled. He was still alive and helpless, yet he smiled, as he realized the power he had over his persecutor: all he had to do was to let her think that she no longer had a hold over him. He could never erase her from his thoughts through willpower alone, she knew that by now. But what if he pretended that he no longer knew who she was, because he no longer was quite in his right mind? It was a gamble, but what alternatives did he have? Wait for death? That might put him on an equal footing with Zephira, but he would no longer be able to get back into his body and take Alex and Judy back to life. Was that what the woman intended him to do by throwing his hair to the wind? He turned his eyes to her for an answer. But silence was all she could give him now, as she lay there immovable, her eyes forever fixed on her broken comb.

38

THE TWO DOGS were sitting on their hind legs right where he had left them. When they saw Lukas come out of the mausoleum, they bared their teeth and snarled, drooling at the mouth. But he could not go back inside and wait for them to go. They would go only when he had breathed his last.

The air was still now, but frosty and cold and filled with snowflakes. That gave him an idea.

His destination was the barge. However, he should not run to it as if he were scared of the dogs. Zephira would be too happy to call him a coward once again. Indeed, he should not even show that he had seen her. So, making as if he had not noticed the barge, he cried: "Oh, almond blossoms, to put on my beloved's head after I comb her hair!"

And he ran about flailing the air with both arms to catch the snowflakes floating in it, the dogs barking and snapping at his heels, as if to call him to order, and his mind thinking: Ach, how low I've sunk! Making such a fool of myself, at my age, to dupe a seventeen-year-old girl! Thus he reached the edge of the water.

Showing neither surprise nor eagerness, he said: "Hi. Would you have a basket?"

Zephira looked at him, perplexed. She was expecting him to beg for the lives of the two bodies she was holding hostage — Lukas did not so much as glance towards them.

"Yes," she finally said. "Come and get it."

"Thank you, thank you," he replied, bowing, again and again, as he waded through the water, the two dogs baying now behind him with frustration. "I'll take the largest basket you have," he added as he climbed on board the barge. "My beloved's hair is very long. It will need lots of almond blossoms."

Zephira scowled.

He smiled. "Where is it — the basket."

Zephira smoldered. "Let's go!"

The barge started to move.

Lukas lost his smile. "No. I must get back to my beloved. Please give me the basket and let me off. Please," he said, thumping his foot. "Please. Please. Please."

"Shut up!" Zephira howled, beside herself now.

Lukas lowered his eyes and whimpered.

The steersman shook his head. "Poor man. His pain has robbed him of his senses. Picking almond blossoms in the fall!"

Soon everything disappeared from sight — the mausoleum, the dogs, the shoreline. The night was dark. The sea, which was as dark as the sky, seemed like a gate into the abyss. Only the crest of a tree was seen sticking up above the water here and there, as if the torrents of rain unleashed by the gulls had drowned the earth as well.

Zephira fixed her dark eyes on him the moment he stepped on board, and would not turn her gaze away. When he wanted to look at her and seek in her beautiful face the sweet and gentle features of the girl he once was so smitten with, he dissembled pouting and frowning, saying now and then: "My beloved will kill you. Just you wait and see. She's stronger than you. And she can fly."

Then he would lapse into moody silences. When his gaze fell accidentally on the two bodies lying at his feet, he would gaze at their open torsos as if they were the floral designs of a rug.

"What's the use now?" the steersman said. "Idiots don't care."

"I'll make him care again," the girl said, finally looking away.

Why? Lukas wanted to scream. She wanted him to be lucid and caring when she tortured him, for maximum effect. He could understand that. But her revenge had been total; what more could she take away from him? His life? Dead he would be as powerful as her, and as vindictive.

He felt despair rise in him again, and he let out a sigh. Instantly Zephira turned and looked at him, as if a sigh were a sign of lucidity. To cover his blunder, Lukas looked up at the snow flakes filling the air and sighed again, saying now: "All those almond blossoms going to waste. Ts-ts-ts."

Now a thick fog came swirling in from all sides and enveloped the barge and its occupants in a mirky dimness.

Should he say something about that? Like: "Try and catch me now! I'm invisible!" Or maybe cry like a child lost in the dark? He decided that, as in everything else, the best thing would be to keep it as simple as possible. So he sighed once more, saying this time: "How is she going to find me now?"

Zephira reappeared through the mist and said to him: "Listen, you coward. There's no other woman. You're mine. Do you understand? I'm your only beloved."

Lukas shook his head. "No you're not. My beloved never yells at me."

39

WHEN THE FOG lifted again, the barge was docked in front of a door.

"Come along," the girl said, opening the door. "Come and get your basket."

They walked down a long corridor, Zephira leading the way with that haughty gait and voluptuous swinging of the hips that were once the object of so many of Lukas's youthful fantasies and ardent desires.

In the corridor they passed many doors. The doors were open and in every room there was a bed and on every bed there was a cat sitting in the position of the Sphinx, its skull wide open. A white-clad doctor was bent over every skull, studying the cat's brain. All was silent, except for the continuous sound of running water.

They went through another door. Zephira glanced over her shoulder to make sure Lukas was following. He too wanted to look over his shoulder, to see if the man behind him had brought along the bodies of Alex and Judy, but he was afraid it would reveal his shamming.

In this corridor, white-clad doctors and nurses padded out of one room and into another. In one room, a doctor was sliding the body of a girl into the disc compartment of a DVD player. In another, a doctor pulled a baby out of its mother's womb, then cut off its nipples and laid them on a plate. In the next room, a team of doctors were discussing whether they should smash a woman's knees to prevent her from running away during the operation. The woman begged them not to do that, swearing that she would not run away.

"Curare!" someone shouted in another room where some soldiers were forcing a man to lie still. "They've injected me with curare!"

They went through another door. Again Zephira glanced over her shoulder to make sure Lukas was following.

There were no doors in this corridor, only walls made of glass. Behind the glass, young men in army fatigues shuffled up and down, talking to themselves, or stood listlessly against the walls, staring at some image which they alone could see.

They went through another door and entered a large ward. Corpses were lying on tables, on stretchers and in boxes everywhere, and a thick cloud of smoke from burning incense floated in the air.

"Wait here," Zephira said to Lukas, then walked away.

The ward's attendants were all sitting at a long table, eating and conversing in a hush. Now and then they glanced towards Lukas and giggled.

Pretending that he was following with his eyes a fly hopping from corpse to corpse, he looked about, and soon his gaze met his son-in-law's.

Alex was lying on a stretcher. His heart was still beating inside his open abdomen, and his eyes were fixed on his father-in-law, tears flowing from them.

How he must hate me, Lukas thought. If only he could make him a sign of recognition or reassurance. At least he knew that Alex was close by and alive. Judy should not be far.

Suddenly his son-in-law averted his eyes and stared in horror at the fly. It was hovering now over his open chest. Finally, it landed on his heart and Alex's head rose in agony, his eyes begging his father-in-law to chase the fly. But how could Lukas chase it without exposing himself, should Zephira be watching?

He started to cough, as if the thick incense floating in the air was choking him. As he coughed, he flapped his arms wildly about — what the hell: he was supposed to have lost his mind — and managed to shoo the fly off Alex's heart. Then he looked away, taking deep breaths and praying that his son-in-law had divined his strange behaviour. But the damn fly was now buzzing around his own head. He drew back in revulsion, flapping his hands before his face, as if the fly were about to discharge on him all the blood it had licked so far. The fly simply flew away and landed on Alex's heart again. And again Alex's head rose in agony, and he looked towards his father-in-law for help. But Lukas gave him none. How could he without arousing Zephira's suspicions? Ach, why did he shoo the fly away from him? Just the thought of it gorging itself on Alex's wound was enough to truly drive him crazy. Desperately, he tried to find some other way to chase it, when Aris's father appeared before him. He was wearing a butcher's apron and brandishing a long butcher's knife.

"I'm going to enjoy this," he said, fondling the blade and testing its edge by slicing a piece of liver off a corpse. "Killing my son with your dreams!"

"Basket!" was all that Lukas could say to him.

This time, as he said it, he wondered if shamming insanity was a good strategy.

"I hope you have enough cash on you to pay for this," Aris's father said, chewing on the piece of liver, blood trickling down his chin on to his apron. "Medical insurance cards are not accepted here." Then he grabbed Lukas by the arm, and pushed him through a door.

40

ZEPHIRA WAS SEATED at a desk similar to the ones they had in primary school. Silently she gazed at Lukas. He stood before her, his head on one side, staring back into her face with an expression of imbecile exasperation. Finally she said: "Never have I wanted anyone as much as I wanted you. When I moved to Lakki, not a day would go by I wouldn't remember you in my prayers."

He was expecting her to explode and give vent to the old grievances that were gnawing at her inside, putting into them all the fury of which she was capable. Instead, she addressed him with no scorn or menace in her voice, only tenderness, nostalgia, and deep sorrow. To cover his dismay, he thumped his foot.

"Basket! You promised!"

"Oh, the love I had for you," she continued, ignoring his tantrum. "In return you spurned me. And because you spurned me, I left the island, and never again would I know happiness. And every day I would think of you and how happy I would have been had you not spurned me. That was my life."

Could one small act of cowardice have such disastrous effects? Should he feel responsible for her failed life? Or was it a ploy to break through his shamming?

"When that life ended," she went on, "what did I see? The boy who had condemned me to such a life, he for whom I was cursed to have no one to close my eyes, never gave me one thought, never felt the slightest remorse."

Tears trickled down her cheeks. Now Lukas had to summon all his strength to go on braving her sad eyes without telling her how much he had loved her and suffered for it. She could not possibly know for she was alive at the time. She had to know, however, that he had embarked on his dream precisely to make amends. Why did she make as if she did not know that?

"Never —" she added, brushing away the tears, "and that's what rankles me most — never even spoke a word of me to anyone. As if I had never existed!"

He was burning to tell her why he had never spoken of her, if only to put a stop to this torture. But more than his life was at stake here. Because even if he told her that he was lucid and willing to submit to the affliction she had decreed for him, he was convinced that she would keep Aris and Judy hostage to hold him to his promise. So, to cut off all compassion, he brought to his mind's eye the fly gorging on his son-in-law's heart because a girl with whom he only shared the memory of a first love did not have the life she wanted and, by virtue of the pains she had suffered, believed herself entitled to the pain she had caused to so many.

"You promised!" he simply groaned, rocking himself backwards and forwards. "You promised!" he repeated, without dropping his eyes from hers, convinced that only this way would he manage to save Alex and Judy and himself. "You promised!"

The girl sighed. "Once a coward always a coward," she said, trying to upset him now with offensive remarks by challenging his pride as a man. "Your father calls you — you run and hide in your bed. Your cowardice bothers you — you blame your mother for sending your father. Now you hide in insanity. But I'll cure you of it yet."

He faltered for a moment as if what she had said was too painful to hear. Fortunately, the girl was busy opening the notebook lying before her and did not notice the pained look in his eyes.

"Let's start from the beginning," she said.

Her head bowed over the page, she wrote with the slowness and application of a schoolgirl, mouthing every word: "*She weeps bitterly in the night, and she has no one to comfort her. All her lovers have dealt treacherously with her; they have become her enemies.*"

She stopped.

"Does enemies take one n or two n's?"

She reflected, her eyes fixed on the page, as if waiting for him to tell her.

"I think it's two n's," she concluded, as her hand searched blindly all over the desk for the eraser. And as blindly, upon reaching it, pushed it over the edge and down to the floor.

A groan rose in Lukas's throat. What was she up to now?

The girl raised her eyes off the page and gave him the command he had been dreading: "Pick up the eraser."

A murderous rage swelled inside him. All he had to do was to jump on her and shut her eyes. But if that could free him from her hold, could it save his son-in-law and Judy as well? So he checked himself once again, and inasmuch as his rage allowed it, he said: "Eraser?"

"The thing that fell off the desk!" she cried out, running out of patience. "Pick it up!"

"No! Basket!"

"You'll have the basket after you pick up the eraser."

"Now! You promised! Now! Now! Now!"

"Plant him!" the girl yelled above his cries.

Four strong arms lifted Lukas off the floor and carried him away.

41

THEY SAT HIM in a chair. Two male nurses. One tied his hands, the other tied his legs.

The first, once he had finished, leaned over his face and said: “You should have loved her.” Then he vanished from his field of vision.

The second nurse said: “If your sanity doesn’t grow back, think of mummification. Have you considered it? It protects the body from decomposition to allow the soul to live in it again.”

“Basket!” Lukas told him. “She promised!”

The nurse shook his head, then moved away.

Lukas took stock of his surroundings. He was inside a large greenhouse. Its floor was plowed in neat, evenly spaced parallel rows. Along each row heads stuck out of the earth, green with moss, about a metre one from the other. Heads of men, buried alive up to the neck. The chair Lukas was sitting on was standing alongside the last row. It was the only row with no heads. The second nurse was standing right in the middle of it. He planted his foot on a shovel and stamped it into the ground, lifted a shovelful of earth, then drove the shovel into the ground again. Obviously he was digging a hole for him. This shamming business was definitely a bad strategy.

He looked at the heads. They were all facing the other way. Who were they anyway? Were they the lovers who had dealt treacherously with Zephira? Whatever, the hole was now one meter deep, and if he did not come up with another strategy soon he would be buried among them.

He thought a moment, then said as if to himself: "Lying witch. I know why she wouldn't give me the basket. She's jealous. Yes. She's jealous of you, my love, because you still turn heads and she doesn't."

Pause.

"Who's he talking to?" one head said to its neighbour.

"My breathtaking beauty of seventeen," Lukas said. "She who makes me fly every time she combs my hair."

Pause.

"A girl is visiting him?" some heads said, their eyes big with anticipation scanning the greenhouse floor. "Where is she?"

"Here," Lukas said, tapping on his heart with his tied wrists. But no one could possibly see his gesture because the heads could not turn more than ninety degrees. "Squatting before my loving eyes, in her pretty short skirt, to comb my hair again."

A loud moan rose from the earth. "She's squatting in his face? Is she wearing panties?"

"Don't cry, my love," Lukas went on. "I'll kill that shrew, I'll take her basket, I'll fill it with almond blossoms, then — show her, Josephine. Show her with your lips every part of her young, curvy, luscious body I'm going to adorn with almond blossoms."

"He has *two* broads visiting him?" the heads cried out. "We're not even allowed a priest!"

"Yes, start with the mouth, Josephine."

There was a hush, as the men strained their ears and threw back their heads to hear the rest.

"How come we don't hear the girls?" someone whispered.

Another replied: "Josephine has put her lips on the girl's, and they're exchanging tongues, stupid!"

"Now her pretty little ears," Lukas went on. "She likes that, eh. Down the hollows of her throat now ... Under her armpits ... Follow the underside of her full, firm, pert breasts ... That's it, all the way up to her nipples ... They're so hard! And sensitive! Blow on them softly and flick each one with the tip of your tongue. Yes, blow and flick. Blow and flick."

Deep sighs and groans were heard now across the floor, interrupted by fits of heavy panting and loud expirations, and finally a cry — "Please! Send them to the front! I want to look too!" — picked up by all the others.

"Now hike her skirt up," Lukas continued, unperturbed. "Oh, those glorious peachy bottoms! Lay them softly on the ground, Josephine — softly! Now ease her long, elegant legs apart ... Don't be shy, my love. No one's looking. Let Josephine pull your panties to the side. That's it."

By now Lukas had aroused so much lust and curiosity that the men were screaming wildly and threatening never to speak to him unless he sent the girls to the front. "We want to see Josephine fingering the girl through her panties!" they said. "We want to see her parting the lips of her tight pussy and chewing on her clit!"

Even the nurse stopped digging to listen to the play by play account of Lukas's fantasy.

"Easy, Josephine, with those rosy petals ... Josephine! Good god! She's buried her face in my love's honeypot and she's lapping her honey like a starved puppy! Look at that tongue licking the honeypot from top to bottom and all round the rim. Josephine, for heaven's sake! Stop pulling her love button into your mouth, you'll bite if off!"

Now the men's cries grew so deafening, the obscenities they screamed became so outrageous that the nurse turned on the sprinklers, shouting: "Quiet, you idiots! There are no girls here!"

But the heads did not believe him. "Send them to the front!" they shouted back. "We want to see the little bitch spread her pink!"

This further excited the men and some begged for mercy. "I can't take it anymore!" they shouted to the nurse. "Smash my head with your shovel, for pity's sake!"

The sprays of water calmed some. The others received a blow on the head with the shovel, but it was a blow administered only as medicine, to knock them out and silence them. But there were so many that as soon as the nurse knocked out a few, some of the others regained consciousness and started howling again and begging for a more violent blow to their head, until Zephira's voice exploded suddenly above the din:

"Give that pimp his cursed basket and get him out of my sight! I don't ever want to see him again!"

Alex and Judy were standing next to her, their abdomens all sewed up.

42

ALEX AND JUDY led him through a door and down a dark staircase. They descended cautiously, Lukas still clutching his basket against his chest, for he was convinced that Zephira had let them go only to see how he would behave with his two companions. Why else would she also release her two hostages and lose her only hold on him?

When they reached the bottom of the staircase, they found themselves facing an ironbound door. Judy turned the latch and the door opened onto a narrow corridor with no doors or windows, which conducted them to another ironbound door. Judy turned the latch, the door opened, and they emerged on a dimly lit, deserted subway platform. As they did, a swirl of music filled the air with the sweet sound of a lyre playing the opening bars of the song to which

Lukas had danced with Zephira the last time he saw her alive.

Unfurl the sails, steer the wheel;
My soul's starved for Leros's mountains,
And my heart for my beloved's lips.

Alex and Judy looked at Lukas to see if he recognized the song that had always given him goose bumps and moved him to tears.

"Blossoms," he told them. "Where are they? My love's waiting."

Judy shook her head. "I should have never told him about dreams."

"It's not your fault," Alex said. "You tell your students the same thing, year after year. Has one of them ever tried such a trip?" He gave Lukas a dark look. "Damn old fool!"

A train was now entering the station.

Judy took Lukas's hand and said softly: "Come, let's go find those almond blossoms."

Lukas forced a smile, and all three got on the train and found themselves in a coach car that was as dimly lit and empty as the platform. They took a seat.

The train pulled out of the station, went through a dark tunnel, then emerged in an endless, snow-covered, flat landscape. It was still dark, but no longer snowing. Fortunately. Lukas had not the slightest desire to make a scene to be let off the train to fill his basket with snowflakes. All he could think of now was a way to save his two companions.

Ensconced in their comfortable chairs and lulled by the roll of the train, Alex and Judy soon gave in to their desire for rest and dozed off. They were as lightly dressed as Lukas, yet they seemed comfortably warm, while he was shivering. Was it because his life was coming to its end? In that case, he had better do something before he too was overcome by his desire to rest, and never woke again. If only he could be sure Zephira was hiding on the train to spy on him.

He decided to dissemble sleep, and soon he saw from beneath his lowered lids a pair of eyes staring at him through the misted-up porthole of the door facing him, at the other end of the centre aisle.

He got up, softly so as not to awake the others, then, still clutching the damn basket, he turned to the door.

The eyes had vanished.

He opened the door. The vestibule was empty. He opened the door facing him, crossed the corridor connection, opened another door. As it clanged shut behind him, he entered a sleeping car. Its narrow aisle was lined on one side with panoramic windows, and on the other with sleeping compartments. There was not a soul anywhere and all the compartment doors were closed. He knocked on the first one, pretending to be looking for almond blossoms, and from behind the door came a woman's voice:

"Come in, my joy."

It was Yolanda's voice.

Should he open the door? He wanted very much to tell his wife that he was still hers. But what if it was a trap?

He knocked on the second door.

Again he heard Yolanda's voice: "Come in, my joy."

He knocked on every other door, and every time he heard Yolanda's voice: "Come in, my joy."

As the train rolled on in the night he went through another corridor connection and entered another sleeping car. Here too there was not one soul, all the doors were shut, and every time he knocked on one, he heard his wife's voice: "Come in, my joy."

Was this part of Zephira's trap, or was his sanity trickling away along with his body heat?

He crossed another corridor connection, the door clanged shut behind him, and he found himself inside a car as dark as the night outside the windows. He felt around him with his free hand. There were no doors here, only seats and tables, on both sides. It was the dining car.

Trailing his free hand over the backrests and table edges to direct himself, he moved on until he noticed a shaft of light on the floor at the other end. Was it escaping from under a door? He moved towards it, reached it, felt for the latch. As soon as he found it, the door flew open, and he found himself standing before the void. He uttered a low cry of surprise and was about to jump back with fright, when in a flash he changed his mind. Only his life could be at stake, he told himself, and to him, at this moment, Alex and Judy were worth it.

"Blossoms!" he cried. And he let himself fall off the train and on to the snow-covered tracks.

43

DEEP SILENCE REIGNED around. Ice had gripped everything. The receding tail lights of the train were the only sign of life. Zephira could not both be on and off the train at the same time, he reasoned. She would follow him, and Alex and Judy would escape. On the other hand, if the eyes spying on him through the porthole and Yolanda's voice behind those doors were the hallucinations of a dying mind, he was doomed to freeze to death in the wilderness, with no one to shut his eyes. Like Zephira.

He scrambled to his feet. Like a dog emerging from water, he shook off the snow filling every crease of his clothes and shoes. Just then she appeared, moving towards him with her haughty, slow-measured gait.

"Fill your basket," she said. "Your beloved is waiting."

She stooped, scooped some snow. Then, with a slowness and an intensity worthy of a sacrament, she lifted her cupped hands over the basket and let the flakes trickle between them, saying as they fell: "A footprint on the snows of time. Tomorrow it will snow again, and she'll be gone. Is that what you thought?"

Chilled to the bone, he rubbed his body with his hands, casting a quick glance past her.

He could still see the tail lights of the train.

"That night," she went on, scooping up more snow, "I was ready to tear my heart out of my chest, if you had asked for it. And what did you do?"

Again she lifted her cupped hands over the basket and let the flakes trickle between them.

"If you could only remember and acknowledge how you scarred me for life." She turned her gaze to him again. "It's hard, Lukas, to be forgotten and not be able to forget. The earth weighs on you. Oh, how it weighs on you, even if you've acquired the resignation of rocks."

He felt his strength ebbing. He would not be able to hold back much longer the feelings she was stirring in him again, or resist the cold that was slowly numbing his flesh and dulling his senses. He cast another glance past her.

This time she noticed. She turned swiftly to look back, and a tremor passed over her face: the tail lights of the train had vanished in the icy night.

When she turned her gaze back to him, there was a fierce frown upon her forehead.

"I never forgot you," he finally said, the only trace of warmth left now in his body being the thought that Alex and Judy were on their way to safety. "For years you lived more in me than anyone had ever done."

She restrained her rage with difficulty. "Don't break my heart again with lies and deception."

"How could I forget you, Zephira? You're my youth."

Her face relaxed slightly, her sorrow appeared to be lightened a little, while he tried to control as best as he could the violent spasms shaking his whole being.

"I better take you back to your body."

Once again he checked his dismay. Was she truly going to let him off that easily?

"But first, you must promise —"

"As often as I listen to a song from Leros, think of the sea, or eat a fish, I shall do it in memory of you."

"Maybe — for a a week or two. Then your grandchild will be born, and you'll think of nothing else." She dropped her gaze, and coyly added: "I want you to leave everything — your family, your business — and retreat to a monastery."

"A monastery."

"Yes, I want you to think only of the lost dream of love that for forty years I went to bed with, and paint icons of me."

Not only did she look forty years younger than her real age, she still thought the way girls used to think back in Leros, forty years ago.

"I'm the only one who loves you now. All others hate you. Your parents. Your grandparents. Your friends. Your daughter.

Your wife. Surely you're gone from her heart now that she knows that you're mine. No need to think about her any more. I don't think about any man but you."

He looked at the girl standing before him as judge and arbiter of his destiny, and told himself that no, there would be no peace for him so long as her eyes were open on the world to which she no longer belonged. But how could he now hurl himself upon her and shut them? Not only had she grown so mistrustful that she would brace herself for such an assault, his feet were buried in deep snow, his hands were growing numb, even his vision was becoming blurred.

"I'm no painter," he said, trying to quell the panic rising in him. "However, I know some painters. I also know poets, and songwriters —"

"I don't want others to give me what you owe me. You came to make amends, didn't you? Here's your chance." All trace of coyness had vanished from her face. "I will not let myself be turned into an anecdote that you circulate from client to client. I want you to bless my memory and revere me as a martyr. I've suffered enough to merit that. And be warned: Here, once a pledge has been given, there's no going back."

"Have mercy on me, Zephira," he said, his arms folded across his chest as if to prevent himself from falling apart. "Impose some other penance. If I make you live again as you want me to, I won't have a life anymore."

"You'll still have the sun — the good sun. You'll have spring and summer and fall. You'll have the taste of cherries and peaches. The smell of jasmine and gardenias and freshly baked bread. You'll have the chirping of the birds. The laughter of children and women and men — that most beautiful of sounds. And, most of all, you'll have the assurance that the icons you paint of me will forever win you a place in the hearts of men and women."

But not in the heart of his wife, who was dearer to him than the smell of freshly baked bread. Nor in the heart of his daughter, who was dearer to him than the sun. Not in the heart of his grandchild either, whose laughter — that most beautiful of sounds, as she called it — she was condemning him never to hear so he could secure with icons that prayers were said for her in perpetuity. But it was pointless to haggle any further. She was convinced that he had robbed her of forty years of happiness, and she would not be appeased unless he compensated her with those he had left.

"And you better start as soon as you get back," she said.

"Be reasonable," he pleaded, to give himself time to think. "I'll have to sell my business first. How else could I buy all the material for the icons?"

"Okay. You may have one week."

He did not have to shake his head — it shook by itself. Even his speech was becoming disjointed, as he said: "A week. I may as well give it away."

"Set it on fire. The insurance will pay."

"Jesus."

With trembling hands, he took off his jacket.

"What are you doing?"

"Life hasn't been easy for me either, you know. But what's the use of raking up the past? Life's good now. And what took me forty years to build, I refuse to destroy and leave nothing to my loved ones, because I made a mistake when I was seventeen."

His legs giving way under him, he tried to unbutton his shirt, but his fingers were too stiff. So he tore it open.

"What the hell, I can't fight always. I know when I'm whipped."

He took his shirt off.

"Could you undo my pants? I don't want to keep anything on when they bury me. All my clothes smell of fish. I'm not a fish."

Surely, she could not mistrust someone who was dying, he told himself. And he would shut her eyes as she undid his pants. But Zephira did not move. She silently scrutinized him. Was she deliberating on some compromise, or trying to guess his ulterior motive?

"Please, undo my pants," he said once more, praying she would do as he said before he turned into ice. "My fingers are too stiff."

Still she would not move. "All I want is to be remembered and loved," she said.

With great effort he checked himself, for her wrath was easily rekindled. Then, as softly as the chattering of his teeth allowed it, he said:

"I can't go back, Zephira. Not only have you robbed me of my memories, you're robbing me of my hopes as well."

"I'm your hope. Your only hope. You should live for me."

He wanted to reply that he was too old to be turned into an object of ridicule — retreating to a monastery to paint icons of her! It would be better, a thousand times better and wiser, to lie on the snow and end it all there.

But what would be the use? The dead are only interested in one thing. He had learned that at the cost of his life. So, he said: "I could never think only of you, Zephira, unless I joined you here. I may still appear seventeen in your eyes, but back there I'm no longer seventeen. And only the love of my family and friends can ease the afflictions of aging. Death is a blessing compared to the torments that you've decreed for me."

He tried to undo his pants himself.

Tears sprung from the girl's eyes. "I don't want you to die," she said. "There's nothing here but memories, and you'll hate me. I don't want you to hate me."

She stood there, looking as helpless as she and Lukas had been at seventeen, on that Leros seashore, when their hearts were filled only with yearnings and possibilities. But Lukas was no longer seventeen. He waded forward through the snow. When he reached her, he did not hurl himself upon her. He enfolded her in his arms and pressed her head against his shoulder.

"Forgive me."

She raised her face towards his. Her eyes were full of tears; her lips swollen and trembling. He looked at them and said: "My youth."

The girl shut her eyes, and everything went black.

44

"YOUR HUSBAND IS alive," the doctor said. "Sit down, please."

She sat down.

Outside, the sun was rising, gilding the snow-covered rooftops across the street.

He's not dead, she told herself, filled with new hope. He's not dead, she repeated, the words resonating now throughout her body. He's alive, she wanted to shout while the doctor, neither his face or voice betraying any emotion, went on talking about how carbon monoxide enters the bloodstream through the lungs and forms a compound that inhibits the blood's capacity to carry oxygen to the organs and tissues. The older the victim, the more vulnerable he is, especially if he is a heavy smoker, he added, using words like carboxyhemoglobin and intubated and stabilized and mechanical ventilation and brain edema.

Rather than ask him what they meant, she glanced towards Irene and Alex and Marcel. Cheer up, she wanted to shout to them. He's alive. And if he's alive, my Lukas will make it. But the words never left her mouth. She remembered the sleeping pill and she bit her underlip to hold them back. How could Lukas make it if his intention was to die?

"No bowel sounds," the litany went on. "Not a growl. Pupils still in mid-position and unreactive. Heart too weak to pump effectively. Blood could back up his venous system."

Yes — whatever that means — but he's still alive. She could feel his body next to hers again, in their bed, his skin as smooth as hers, and much warmer. So warm he could heat up the bed sheets within minutes. My sexy, portable heater, she used to call him. Now she made a vow: after he gets out of here and she has explained to him what she had truly done the night before, she would take him to that mountain, find the same bench, and exchange with him another one of those kisses sweet and deep and certain as the desire to live. Even if it is minus twenty. He will keep her warm.

The buzz had stopped, and the doctor's voice became clearer, sharper. Now she could make out an entire sentence:

"It's only reasonable that we should start thinking of organ harvest."

"Harvest? What does that mean?"

He handed her a driver's licence. Lukas's driver's licence.

"Look at the back, please. He agrees, in case of accident, to donate his organs."

"Why are you telling me this? He's still alive, isn't he?"

"Yes. But as I just explained to you, he's unresponsive to all stimuli, is unable to breathe without assistance, has no spontaneous movements, and he appears to have lost all brain stem reflexes. At the moment, all that is left for me to suggest is life support. And consideration of organ harvest."

"I don't understand. He's still alive ..."

"We tried everything, yet there have been no neurologic changes."

"He's been here only — what, three, four hours?"

"We've tried everything," he repeated, checking his clipboard, so as not to see the look of terror in her eyes and to give time for his request to sink in.

"There must be something!"

Her eyes were sharp again, sharp and fully alert. The doctor, on the other hand, was now rubbing his, as if to fend off sleep.

"Maybe," he said, trying hard to maintain an expression of cool dispassion. "Maybe not."

"What does *that* mean?"

"A miracle."

"Then we'll wait for a miracle."

She put her husband's driver's licence into her purse, as if to underline her command. Then she turned towards Alex, who was a dentist, to tell him that she wanted a second opinion, from a doctor who was older than this young intern and fully awake.

"I know this is hard," the young doctor was saying now. "But, think, please, of your husband's wish. If he agreed to donate his organs, I'm sure he'd also agree with what I'm about to say. Once you get past the shock, it will make sense to you as well. Your husband is breathing still, yes. And he's breathing right now forty percent oxygen — twice that of room air. Still, his blood saturation is barely adequate."

"What the hell does that mean?" she cried out. And she turned again towards Alex for help. Surely he would know how to put all this jargon into words she could understand.

Two seconds later Alex was by her side, as exhausted and heavy-eyed as the young doctor. She reached out and took his hand. Her son-in-law returned her squeeze. Then he said: "The brain is extremely vulnerable to oxygen deprivation. He could be kept on life support for weeks, months. But even if he wakes again, chances are he'll have permanent brain damage."

Her hand slipped away from Alex's and shot up to her mouth.

"Meanwhile," the doctor added, "without blood flow to the coronary arteries, every minute that passes could result in the death of a few more myocardial cells and reduce the likelihood his heart would function in a recipient's chest. It would be a pity. We have a seventeen-year old patient who's been waiting eight months for a heart. Your husband's is the best match that's come up for her. Believe me, this is not premature."

She took a deep breath. "How much longer can we wait before the heart becomes unusable?"

"You aren't really expecting a miracle?"

"How much longer can we wait?" Alex said.

"An hour? Two, at the most."

She lowered her head, all the strength bled out of her. But not her rage. Rage towards herself for caring about what everyone might think of her while her husband was dying; rage towards Voula, not because she tried to shame her, but because she called Irene. If she ever loses her baby, she thought, I'm going to kill her. She wanted to turn to her daughter, tell her at least not to remain standing, in her condition, but she was afraid to look her in the eyes.

"Give us a few minutes, please," Alex said to the doctor.

"Sure."

As she thought of the undying hatred that her daughter would nurse towards her for the rest of her life, once again she heard a buzz. But this time the buzz was not in her head. It was that of an alarm overhead. She realized it when the doctor, who was about to leave them alone, sprinted down the reception area and pushed through the double doors into the corridor. By the time she reached the corridor, Alex, Irene and Marcel trotting after her, she had the feeling that the hospital's entire medical personnel had sprung into action and were thronging the trauma room where Lukas's body, if not his mind, was desperately trying to cling to life. But as she stood in the doorway, peering apprehensively inside, Yolanda had eyes only for the doctor, as he checked the cardiac monitor screen whose blips now followed the electrical pattern of a dying heart, while an intern held an anesthesia mask to Lukas's face, manually pumping oxygen into his lungs.

The pattern of a heart racing to stay ahead of death, she wondered, or striding towards it?

A moment later, numb with terror, she watched the doctor slap the defibrillator paddles on Lukas's chest.

"Two hundred joules," he shouted.

The burst of electricity shot through Lukas's body, jolting every muscle into one spasm. He gave a grotesque jerk, then he lay still again.

"Two hundred and fifty!"

There was another jolt, another grotesque spasm, then Lukas's body collapsed once again.

How distant he appeared now. As distant from her as the stars of the night.

Her gaze blurred with tears.

"Four hundred!"

The words resonated like the sound of her life being ripped in two. She wanted to turn away, but felt too drained to move. So she shut her eyes, convinced now that it was all done not to save her husband's life as much as his heart and other usable organs. And she was about to tell them to stop torturing him and let him die in peace when, as everyone else was about to step away from the doctor while he applied the paddles once again, she heard someone say: "I'm getting a pulse!"

45

WHEN LUKAS CAME out of his coma, he found himself stretched out on a hospital bed, surrounded by a thicket of plastic tubes and IVs. Yolanda was at his side.

"What am I doing here?" he said. "What happened?"

"You're asking *me*?"

"I was in the garage, parking the car."

She could almost hear her own heart cry with relief. Her husband showed no signs of brain damage, or any of the after-effects of severe CO poisoning, such as confusion and memory loss. She wanted to call her daughter and break the news to her, but she wanted to verify one thing first.

"You parked the car in the garage. Then what did you do?"

He lowered his eyes.

"There was a bottle of sleeping pills on the front seat."

He looked at his wife again.

"Do you remember taking a sleeping pill?"

A blush appeared on his face. "Yes."

"Do you remember leaving the motor of your car on?"

He frowned. "Why would I do such a stupid thing?"

She shrugged, half-relieved. "You tell me."

Silence.

Finally, Yolanda said the words burning her tongue: "Why did you take a sleeping pill?"

He cleared his throat. "Could I have a cigarette?"

"You must be joking."

"Call the doctor. He'll understand."

"First he'll ask you the same questions. The police too."

He raised an eyebrow.

"They have to investigate such incidents. Don't you think I deserve to know before they do?"

He told his wife why he took the sleeping pill. His motive sounded so preposterous that Yolanda believed him.

She said: "I don't know if I should laugh, or tear your head off."

Then:

"Did you find her?"

Pause.

"I don't know."

Like Lazarus, when he returned from the kingdom of the dead, he had no memories of what he saw. As if Charon had given him a potion of forgetfulness before allowing him to return to the land of the living.

"If you decide to try again," Yolanda said, "please, do it in our bed."

Then she called her daughter.

"Forgive me," Irene said to her mother. "I lost my head. When I heard that you were out that night —"

"It's all right."

"It's not all right. I'm going straight to Voula's, and nail her tongue myself."

"You'll do nothing of the sort. She saved your father's life."

After she hung up, Yolanda told her husband what Voula had done. Then she asked him what he thought of Daniel Bouchard's proposition.

He replied: "It's not for me to say. If you want to do it, do it. Whatever the outcome may be, it could never be worse than the regret you'll feel one day for not having done it."

Yolanda smiled, then said: "I hope the cops will buy your cockeyed story."

The two officers had heard worse. And they had other, more serious fish to fry than a crazy old Greek who wanted to visit the dead in his dreams. As they got up to leave, Lukas suddenly saw in his mind's eye soldiers forcing a man to lie still on an operating table.

Obviously even Charon has no soothing potion of forgetfulness, and no dream entirely disappears. At first the individual images were so disparate that they made no sense. A doctor bent over the open skull of a cat, studying its brain. Mussolini drinking from his own belly. A broken comb. It was as if his memory had turned into an ocean and he was bobbing on its surface. Then a charitable flash would illuminate the deep dark waters, and he would glimpse another image. Some images swam in his head like schools of fish, but dispersed and vanished when he tried to approach them. Others stayed like an underwater promontory or a sunken ship. Some of these images were so painful that at first sight, they hit him with the force of a cramp. The only way to relieve the cramp, he discovered, was to dive back into the charted waters of his real past and bring up an anecdote about his parents, grandparents or childhood friends, which he told and retold, embellishing it shamelessly every time.

At first Yolanda lent a patient ear to his yarns, telling herself that he was simply recovering from the shock of his "trip." But soon she noticed other changes, which looked more like the ominous harbingers of senility. For one, after he passed his fingers through his beautiful mane of silvery-white undulating locks, her husband softly blew on his hand now, then silently watched the flight of some hair she did not or could not see. Another sign: before he took his first sip of wine, he now poured a few drops from his glass over the floor. To her the most bizarre sign was — what else could she call it? — his sudden bout of narcissism. Lukas hated having his picture taken. Moreover, his restaurant was so famous that he no longer needed to advertise. Yet on his first day back to work he ordered fifty thousand flyers, with his picture printed on them.

Alarmed, Yolanda consulted a specialist. Who gave her a list of specific signs she should look for and a list of strategies to help her deal with them. "I strongly recommend that one-week trip to Cuba you suggested for spring break," he added.

Lukas refused to go to Cuba. "We should take a whole month, this summer," he said, "and go to Leros."

His staff too noticed a change in Lukas. He was more withdrawn and subdued. And when clients left the restaurant, instead of a parting joke, he would now tell them: "Be good. What we do in life echoes in eternity."

Two weeks after his "trip," Judy Yamada dropped by his restaurant with a book on dreams. And she was astonished when Lukas, who had never refused a good read, would not take it.

"Such things ought to be left alone," he said. "This is a game where the only way to win is to not play."

Two weeks after that, he skipped his monthly poker game. Was it because he could not play poker without his cigarettes? Yolanda had convinced him to quit. "Don't you want to see your grandchild grow up?" she had said. So on poker night he went home instead, and while his wife corrected some papers, he quietly dealt himself a game of solitaire. Yolanda had never seen him play solitaire before. Although she had often wished her husband would spend more evenings at home, she prayed that he would never do that again.

But he had to come home to sleep. And every night since his "trip," sleep, once a merciful ally, had turned into a terror that gripped his heart as the hour approached. He had only told her that he could not, for the life of him, recall how his dream voyage ended. He did not have to tell her also that every night he wondered if Zephira would reappear and how she would behave towards him — his anguish was written all over his face.

The evening her husband spent at home playing solitaire, Yolanda decided that she should do something. The next day, she went to see her daughter and suggested that she give the baby, should it be a girl, the name Zephira.

Irene raised an eyebrow, like her father. Was her mother trying to worm out of her the name she had picked for her baby? Yolanda always claimed that she did not care for the old Greek custom of perpetuating a parent's memory by giving his or her name to your child. Had she lied? Was she secretly hoping that her granddaughter be given her name?

"Who the hell is Zephira?" Irene said. "What kind of a name is that?"

"It's a beautiful name," Yolanda replied. "Even if you've already picked one, a child can have more than one name. Besides, you owe me one."